PANCHO'S PILOT

JACK R. STANLEY

Published by Wrightbridge Press

Quantity sales. Special discounts are available on quantity purchases by corporations, associations, and others. For details, contact the publisher at the address above.

Printed in the United States of America

ISBN: 978-1-947726-59-8

DEDICATION

To the love of my life
Mary Lee
who makes all things possible.

2 Free Ebooks

MURDER IN MULESHOE
There's a killer in town. Do we hunt the S.O.B. down or throw him a parade?

GUNS ALONG THE RIO
Two fresh-off-the-ranch 17-year-olds join the Texas Rangers in 1858. What could possibly go wrong?

Two Free E-books@ http://eepurl.com/dKEi_Y

As always, to the love of my life,
Mary Lee,
who makes all things possible.

CHAPTER 1

The shadow of a 1916 bi-plane drifted over the landscape. The craft's motor clattered as it labored to stay aloft. It was a relatively new craft — a marvel of wood, canvas, and bailing wire. The star insignia on its wing and fuselage marked it as property of the U.S. Army, pre-World War I. On the body and on the wings was the number 13.

The country below was the vast ruggedness of the desert in the Texas Big Bend country. It stretched out for miles and miles under a blistering and relentless sun. The canyons and jagged buttes alternated between patches of flat sand and rock.

The wings dipped, the nose bobbed, and the general path of the plane was less orthodox or even military than that of an inebriated albatross.

The cause of the flight pattern was not the canvas, wood, and wire that held the thing together. It was the pilot.

Barney Lindecker, 23, was dressed in the uniform, leather

cap, and oil-spattered goggles of an Army aviator. He hung over the side of the rear cockpit. His eyes were crossed, his tongue draped from his mouth, and he was holding his forehead with his free hand. He was trying, with only partial success, not to look at the ground several hundred feet below. By the look of him, it was clear that in his heart he lusted for death.

The plane circled lower and lower but flew on, making some progress in the same general direction — south.

The low flying craft approached a ranch which sat alone in the barren country. It was not much of a ranch, but there was a ranch house, barn, corral, windmill and stock tank. The plane drifted toward the barn and looked as if it might hit it.

Something caused Barney to look up from his praying to die in time to see the barn looming before him. He jerked the stick to one side and closed his eyes.

The De Havilland veered to one side and cleared the structure --- but only by inches. The plane zoomed over the stock pond and almost took out the windmill before it began to rise in the air once more.

As the plane zoomed over the stock pond, a figure rose out of the water. It was the strikingly shapely figure of a young women.

Addie Etheridge was 20 and wore only her birthday suit (and on her it looked great).

Barney opened one eye to see if he was dead or alive. What he saw as he looked behind the plane made him open both eyes as wide as they'd go.

Addie was an attractive young woman with a big friendly smile. She waved at Barney.

Barney started to smile but he couldn't; he gagged trying to keep his breakfast down. He and number 13 flew on.

Addie watched as the plane took another dip toward the ground then abruptly lifted back into the sky. She grabbed her towel and started climbing out of the pond.

⊗⊗⊗

CANDELILLA PLANTS AND BEAR GRASS GREW AROUND THE edge of a placid water hole amid boulders and sand. A saddled contentedly grazing horse was tied to a bush. Farther on there was the shadow of someone back in the bushes.

The man's strained voice was heard.

"Oh, come on, damn it!!"

It was Lurty Etheridge. He was a 60-year-old cowboy/rancher who squatted amid some of the rocks, his pants pulled down, answering an important call of nature.

There was also movement in the undergrowth. More than one man was sneaking toward Lurty, who remained focused on his task.

CHAPTER 2

Emiliano, a Mexican bandit, replete with mustache, several days' growth of beard and a single bandoleer across his chest, led his compadres sneaking through the bush. He carried a rifle in one hand and a Navy Colt revolver in the other. A bowie knife was evident in a scabbard which hung from his belt.

Emiliano looked back over his shoulder and waved two other bandits forward. Through the rocks crawled Beto and Martin.

Beto wore a bandoleer but it was totally devoid of shells. He carried a Winchester rifle with a busted stock. Beto's smile was painted with broken and decayed teeth. His speech revealed his almost complete lack of brains.

Martin was the thinnest of the trio but had narrow threatening eyes. He carried a machete in one hand and a Mauser rifle in the other. Martin stopped to scratch his crotch before he moved on.

When Martin and Beto joined Emiliano, their leader, he

signaled them to spread out, each going in a different direction, circling Lurty and the nearby waterhole.

The sweat of Lurty's effort soaked his face and collar. His tan skin was the result of years in the open. His attitude was the culmination of accumulated frustration and determination.

Lurty had a habit of talking to himself. "I ain't crapped in so long — my eyes are turnin' brown."

He strained again, but to no avail.

The sound of a rock being kicked over brought Lurty suddenly to alert.

As his pale blue eyes darted around, Lurty reached for his pistol on a weathered gun belt which currently hung with his pants — down between his knees and his boots. He stood slightly, his trusty Remington .44 in his hand. He then looked around.

"Who's that! Who's the hell's out there?"

There was no response.

"Damn it, I said who in the hell is that! If'n ya' don't show y'self, I'll shoot th' shit of you!"

Beto ducked down, laughing at what he could see of Lurty.

Lurty heard the motion and turned in the direction of Beto's laugh. Lurty tried to take a step, but he was hobbled by his britches and gun belt. He stumbled. Failing his arms, he tried to get his balance back, but still fell — backwards into the sand and the rocks — and a horse crippler cactus. In the process he managed to fire a shot which ricocheted off a non-offending boulder.

Lurty let out a scream and twisted over to his side in pain.

Emiliano rose and saw Lurty's predicament without smiling. Emiliano simply shook his head. Dumb gringo.

Martin was enjoying Lurty's state with a stupid grin. He stepped into the open and leveled his rifle at Lurty.

By this time Beto was roaring with laughter as he tried to step out into the clear. But he was laughing so hard that he tripped and fell over himself.

Emiliano stood to his full height — and continued to shake his head.

Lurty fumbled away his pistol as he rolled over. His first action was to start pulling cactus needles out of his naked rump.

He got a couple out, resulting in as much pain as the objects inflicted as they went in. After getting a couple of spines out, Lurty looked up at Emiliano, Martin and Beto. The trio approached and stood a few feet away looking down on him.

Martin put away his machete and scratched again.

Emiliano noticed the scratch and was reminded that he had a similar itch. He indulged himself.

Beto was still enjoying the scene playing out in front of him. He slapped his knee with joy.

But a stern look from Emiliano finally encouraged Beto to stifle his laugh. The smile remained.

Finally Emiliano turned back to Lurty.

"Buenos dias, Señor."

Lurty struggled to get to his feet and then to get his pants pulled up. He jerked again when his trousers struck another cactus needle.

"Buenos, your ass!!" he said.

CHAPTER 3

"Don't move, Señor," Emiliano said.

Lurty stopped once his pants were up. He looked defiantly at Emiliano.

Emiliano had his rifle leveled at Lurty. Now, Emiliano smiled.

"We caught the gringo -- how they say -- with his pants down?" Martin said.

Lurty didn't find this humorous in the least.

"What d' ya' want?"

"We are poor peons, Señor. We were hoping you would have some of your gringo money for us."

"Money?" Lurty spat. "Ya' can't get piss out of no rock an' ya' can't get no money out a' me! Ain't got any!"

Emiliano looked to Beto and then at Lurty.

"Not even -- a few silver dollars?"

"Silver dollars? Hell, I had even one silver dollar I'd cut my throat an' die rich."

Martin shook his head. "Estupido gringo!"

Emiliano said, "If you had only one silver dollar — it would be better to spend it — on a bottle...."

"Or a woman," Beto said.

"... then cut your throat. You would still die poor — but happy."

The bandits laughed.

Lurty gave them a "go to hell" look.

Beto, said, "Since he has no silver dollars — maybe he would loan us some of his cows?"

"If you mean stealin', say stealin'!" Lurty narrowed his eyes.

"Señor," Emiliano tried to look shocked, "we are not thieves."

"What d' ya' call it, then?"

"We are — liberators."

Lurty spat in disgust once more.

"Yeah. You're gonna liberate me of my cows."

"Even liberators must eat. We could liberate you of your life, Señor.

Beto found this very funny. But his laughter was cut short by the sound of an approaching airplane. Beto looked around attempting to place the strange sound.

"And our General will not let us come back empty hand-ed," Emiliano continued.

"Your General? You one of Pancho Villa's bunch?"

"Villa?" Emiliano, Martin and Beto all spat. "We ride with Pancho Renteria!"

"Who? Ya' mean that one handed, one-hooked som'bitch? Pancho Gancho?"

"The General doesn't like that name, Señor."

"Then tell him to get himself another hand and quit *liberating* on this side of the border."

Emiliano and Martin had by then also noticed the sound. Emiliano was the first to turn his eyes skyward.

Martin and Beto followed. Lurty, whose hearing was not too great, was the last to look up. His eyes widened as he did.

"¿Qué es?" Beto said.

"It's a — a flying -- auto — auto — mobile," Emiliano said.

Lurty's expression brightened.

"That ain't no automobile. That there's a by God United States Army aeroplane!"

Martin and Beto exchanged worried looks.

Lurty pressed his advantage.

"And all them pilots — they're — crazy — nasty-dangerous — an' mean as hell!"

Up in the air, Barney, the nasty, dangerous, mean-as-hell pilot, was uncontrollably air sick. He closed his eyes. He didn't care where he crashed now. He just hoped it would all be over soon. He leaned over to one side of the cockpit and the craft looped in that direction.

The liberators took aim and fired at the plane just as it looped around. But at the end of the loop the craft headed directly for the waterhole — and them — fast. The bandits fired wildly.

"Now ya' done it! You got him pissed!"

Then the craft was upon them, roaring like a mighty demon.

The bandits got the same idea at the same instant. They dove into the water hole.

Even Lurty hit the dirt as the De Havilland flashed past — but Lurty landed on another cactus needle and screamed as he rolled over.

The bandits came up spitting and gasping as Lurty grabbed his pistol out of the sand.

Lurty stood holding his weapon in one hand, holding up his pants with the other. He stepped over to the edge of the water hole and fired at the bandits.

But the weapon fizzled and popped instead of exploding as it should. Lurty looked disgustedly at his pistol.

The Mexicans realized that Lurty was trying to get the drop on them and they turned on him with their guns. But these weapons were now wet, too, and wouldn't fire at all.

Lurty aimed at the trio and fired again.

This time the gun discharged a round properly and kicked up the water near Emiliano.

Lurty's next shot fizzled again.

The bandits didn't need time to think. They scrambled out of the water and headed for their horses.

Lurty kept firing but only one more round went off correctly. The slug hit a rock and ricocheted with a loud zing.

The bandits got to their horses, leaped into their saddles, and slapped leather getting the hell out of there.

Lurty, convinced he had won a major battle, then burst into laughter. He slapped his side in glee only to locate yet another cactus spine. He flinched in pain and twisted around to pull the sticker out. As he did, he looked up watching the bi-plane fade away in the distance.

CHAPTER 4

Barney, totally unaware of Lurty and the bandits, slumped over in the cockpit as the craft labored on.

An adobe headquarters building, still under construction, had a U.S. and a Texas flag on a flag pole. The solid structure was in marked contrast to the rows of pup tents and a larger mess tent, all of which were pitched in the blowing dust.

A squad of doughboy uniformed soldiers drilled on the open flat dirt. Others continued to work on the adobe building. This was Fort Lajitas on the Texas/Mexican border right on the slow flowing Rio Grande.

The handle "doughboy" came from the dust that covered everyone and everything. The name had evolved from "adobe boys" to "dobe boys" to just "doughboys."

Standing on the porch of the headquarters building was

Lt. Col. Claude Zane. The silver oak leaf on his collar was, like his uniform, somehow immune to dust. Zane wore round, wire-rimmed eye glasses. He had close cropped hair, a neat mustache and wrinkles.

Beside Zane stood Capt. J.J. Rendon, an officer as much out of shape as Zane was in shape. Thirty year old Rendon's uniform appeared to have been made by Omar-the-Tent-Maker.

The sound of an approaching De Havilland was heard. Zane looked up with a scowl.

With the Rio Grande in the background, a half dozen De Havilland bi-planes were parked on the edge of the dirt air strip at the edge of the camp. The craft in the air circled the field camp and lined up on the recently constructed runway.

Rendon checked his clipboard.

"Number 6. That will be Banion, Sir."

"All right. Where the hell is Linedecker?"

Zane crammed a cigar in his mouth and began to chew on it.

"Damn turkey buzzards!" Zane mumbled.

"Sir?" Rendon asked.

"Those damn fool aeroplanes look like turkey buzzards."

"Oh. Yes, Sir."

"What does the cavalry need with turkey buzzards?"

"They are the future of the military, Sir. Like the automobile."

"Huh! I've never yet seen an automobile that can go where a good horse can."

"No, Sir. But then, you don't have to clean up after an automobile — and a horse can't go where an airplane can."

"Captain, you ever see a horse catch fire?"

"Uh — no, Sir."

Zane snorted with satisfaction and headed back into the headquarters building. Over his shoulder he said, "Let me know if and when that slacker Linedecker lands or crashes."

Rendon called after him stopping Zane at the door.

"Linedecker is a good lieutenant, Sir, even if he's not the best pilot we have. I've read his file. He's from a very distinguished military family."

This was of some interest to Zane.

"As a matter of fact," Rendon went on, "I wouldn't be surprised if he managed to — to do something — something heroic. It's the kind of thing that's in his blood."

"Linedecker? I don't care what his family's like, that shave tail will never be anybody's hero. And he's National Guard, too. Like the rest of you. Why the hell do we need any National Guard?"

"We had the planes, Sir, and we were available."

Zane snorted once more.

"Linedecker has a rather strong motivation," Rendon continued.

Zane shot Rendon a questioning glance.

"It's a confidential note in his file. According to that, Linedecker must 'distinguish himself in the service of his country' — or they'll kick him out of the family. And his family is rich."

Zane absorbed this information without comment.

"Shall I send a patrol out to look for Linedecker, Sir?"

Zane turned back to Rendon.

"I'm not about to waste good horseflesh in this God forsaken country looking for — lieutenants in turkey buzzards."

Rendon knew when to shut up. And this was that time. Zane started to go inside but turned back once more.

"If Lindecker isn't back here by -- sunset ...."

"Yes, Sir?"

"Then put that shave tail down as Absent Without Official Leave."

Rendon was surprised by the order.

"A.W.O.L., Sir?"

"Let's see him 'distinguish' himself out of that."

Zane stomped off to his office. Rendon followed calling out, "The afternoon dispatches are on your desk, Sir."

CHAPTER 5

L urty had his pants up and his pistol apart on a flat rock, cleaning it. He was going to be ready the next time *liberators* came to call.

That was when he heard noises in the brush again. He quickly reassembled his Colt and started to reload it. He dropped to his knees as he finished loading and cocked the hammer as he narrowed his eyes.

"Put your hands up an' get your ass out here where I can see ya'!"

"It's just me and Buck, Daddy," Addie called.

From behind some boulders not far away stepped Addie. She wore a work shirt, not buttoned all the way up, riding skirt and western boots. She led Buck, a tired old saddled nag overdue for a date with a flock of buzzards.

Lurty relaxed and stood up.

"Addie? What in th' hell are you doin' out here?"

Addie crossed around the small water hole and over to Lurty. But she really had her eyes on the sky.

"Nothin' — now, I guess."

Addie gave up looking for the plane, sat down on a rock, and took off her boots. Lurty put his pistol away.

"You came all the way out here for nothin'?"

"Ol' Buck didn't seem to mind."

Addie pulled her skirt up and revealed a set of very shapely legs as she waded out into the water.

"You ever think ol' Buck might like a little water?"

Lurty went to the horse and led the animal to the water. While he couldn't make him drink, Buck took care of that for himself.

"Gal, you're jest lucky you didn't get here five minutes earlier."

"Why?"

"There was three honest t' God Mex'can bandits — standin' right over there ready t' blow holes in me."

"No foolin'?"

"I sure as hell ain't!"

"Why didn't they?"

"You sound disappointed."

"Oh, Daddy. I was wonderin' how you got away from them."

"Well, fer one thing these weren't Villa's bunch. They ride with that Pancho Gancho."

"The one with only one hand and a hook?"

"Yup. They're the ones that — had their way with Sue McClellan last month."

Addie got an image in her head and it wasn't all bad. Her hormones were in full bloom and sometimes so was her imagination.

"You never did say what you're doin' out here?"

"I was followin' an aeroplane. But I lost it."

"Follerin' it?"

"It's th' first one I've ever seen."

"Them areoplanes belongs to the Army. And I told you 'bout stayin' away from soldiers."

"Daddy, soldiers and bandits are about the only boys my age we ever have around here."

"Boys are the last damn thing you need."

"Why? I kind of think I'd like to get to know one — or more."

"Cause you don't know nothin' about boys, and I don't want you learnin' it — all at once."

"Then when am I goin' t' learn it?"

"When you're old enough."

"When mother was 16, she was married."

To himself Lurty said, "She was also knocked up." To his daughter he said, "You stay away from them by God bandits."

"Then what's wrong with soldiers? Last month when that bunch come by the ranch, you wouldn't let me even talk to any of 'em."

"Cause I know what's on their minds!"

"Well, maybe it's the same thing that's on my mind."

"That's what worries me!"

Ol' Buck was finished drinking and stood waiting for something to do — or to die. It was hard to tell which.

"Then you learn me something about boys, Daddy."

"Th' first thing is — when you meet boys, make sure you have your clothes on."

Addie smiled and laughed as she noticed her shirt was gaping and she was showing some ample cleavage. She buttoned up another button.

"Oh."

Addie looked up at the sky and remembered.

"That areoplane — it swooped down — graceful like.... It come s' low I could see the driver's face. He's sure cute."

"Come on, get out of there, Addie. I need t' get back t' work. You get back t' th' house."

Addie wiped off her feet and reached for her boots.

"He didn't look too well. I was afraid he was goin' t' fall. When he flew off, I thought I'd better go after him. I wish you'd seen him."

"I did."

Addie brightened. "Really? Where'd he go?"

"The same way he was headed -- south."

"Toward th' border? What if he falls over there?"

"If he does, he'd be in a sure-as-hell pickle."

"I'm goin' after him."

"No, you ain't! You're goin' back to th' house."

"Daddy!!"

"Look at Ol' Buck. He might not even make it home. You try takin' him towards the river and he's liable t' drop dead 'fer you reach the water."

Lurty held up a hand to stop Addie before she could say another thing.

"You get Ol' Buck back home and I'll go see 'bout this here flyboy."

"And if he needs some help?"

Lurty looked down and checked his pistol.

"I guess I can handle anything Pancho Gancho's dealin' out."

CHAPTER 6

Addie beamed as she hugged Lurty.

"Oh, Daddy! You're wonderful!"

Lurty wasn't comfortable with displays of affection. He tried to brush her off.

"You get on home."

Addie managed to kiss his cheek before she backed off.

"All right, all right."

Addie mounted Buck. But she turned to Lurty before she rode out.

"If you can — find out his name."

Lurty frowned as Addie headed home.

To himself Lurty said, "If he's across the Rio, his name is dead."

As Buck and Addie headed away, she turned back in the saddle.

"Daddy? Think there's any chance he saw me? I was out takin' my bath an' when he flew by -- I jumped up and waved at him."

"Gal, if your mama was still alive, she'd die."

"I got a real good look at him, Daddy."

"Then I'll bet he got a real good look hisself."

"You really think he saw me?"

"If he didn't, he's either blind 'r too stupid to fly."

Addie took this as a compliment.

"Thanks, Daddy."

She rode off smiling.

Lurty shook his head. What was a father to do with a girl who's ripe for the picking and yearning to be plucked?

"Dammmmmnnnn! If 'in she weren't my own daughter —."

He slapped himself before he could finish the thought. He bit his lower lip and headed for his own horse.

⚜

BARNEY CONTINUED TO FLY OL' UNLUCKY 13, HOLDING HIS head and slumping back in the cockpit. The plane had gained some altitude, again.

The river wound below through the boulders, sand, and cacti. The shadow of the bi-plane crossed it.

Barney slouched forwards and backwards in the cockpit. He opened his eyes for a moment, looked down and then collapsed back in his seat.

The plane descended as it followed no particular pattern -- unless it's that of a busted duck flying during labor.

As the craft got closer to the ground, Barney forced himself to look down again. He saw something ahead.

The De Havilland approached from the distance and made a pass over a flat wash. The craft came back and landed.

Barney was doing his level best to do what he had learned. He simply wasn't doing it well.

The plane banged into the ground, bounced a couple of times and then stayed on the ground. It rolled to a stop.

Barney sagged back in the cockpit relieved to be on the ground. He flipped a switch on the dashboard to kill the engine and let the prop stop spinning. He jumped as the engine backfired.

He pulled off his goggles and crawled out of the cockpit. He eased himself to the ground not really believing it was real.

Barney quickly discovered that he had trouble walking. He forced himself away from the plane and almost staggered to the shadow of a large rock where he dropped to the ground. He peeled off his cap and said a silent prayer of thanks just for being on the ground and in one piece again.

BACK IN LT. COL. ZANE'S OFFICE EVERYTHING WAS NEAT and austere. Everything was by the book -- military. Even the pencils were lined up from the smallest to the largest.

Zane stood at the window and looked out on the camp the men were still building. He was angry and his face was red with it.

"Capt. Rendon!" he called.

A moment later Rendon entered hesitantly.

"Is Linedecker back?" the Col. said still gazing out the window.

"No, Sir," Rendon said and then added, "— but, Sir --."

"What is it then?"

"About this -- A.W.O.L., Sir."

"What about it?"

"Ah — Linedecker could have had to make an emergency landing. He could have had some mechanical trouble. I mean, pilots do run into all kinds of things. And we have to be careful, Sir. I mean, one of these pilots could end up being some kind of hero — making the whole outfit look good. But if we — ?"

"What is it with you and Linedecker? I've told you he is no hero and from the way he took off, I'm not sure he's even a pilot."

"Beg pardon, Sir?"

Zane turned to Rendon.

"I said, Linedecker is not a pilot. He's not even a lieutenant."

Rendon wasn't following any of this as Zane went on.

"As a matter of fact, Captain, Mr. Linedecker isn't even in the Army!"

Rendon tried to come to terms with what the Colonel was saying but had no success at it.

"I'm sorry, Sir, but I'm lost."

"*That* may be news to you, Captain Rendon, but it certainly isn't to me."

"Sir, are you saying that Lt. — I mean Mr. Linedecker is a — spy?

Col. Zane turned to Rendon.

"He's worse than that. He's a civilian!"

Rendon gave up. This whole conversation was beyond him.

Zane picked up a military dispatch off his desk and handed it to Rendon.

Rendon read the sheet and the fog cleared as he did.

"A clerical error?"

"He was to be discharged — as an enlisted man -- from the National Guard — three months ago."

"Then how did he get in flight school — and graduate?"

"Obviously, illegally. He's a damn civilian!"

Zane snatched the paper back from Rendon and dropped it on his desk.

"Now that civilian is illegally in possession of military property."

"Yes, Sir. But — if he's a civilian — he can't be — A.W.O.L."

Zane shot Rendon a dirty look. The commander didn't like that at all.

CHAPTER 7

From behind some of the rocks which surrounded the dry wash, a sombrero slowly rose until a set of dark, deep-set, eyes became evident. Then a steel hook appeared and chipped into the rock as a whole man rose.

This fat, dirty, bandit king wore two U.S. Army .45 semi-automatic pistols and looked like Pancho Villa's ugly brother. But this was Pancho (The Hook — Gancho) Renteria.

He signaled his men to move in.

Bandits of all sizes, shapes and smells popped up from behind rocks and began converging on the De Havilland. Pancho led the way.

The shadow of Pancho, especially the hook, fell across Barney until the sun was completely blocked out of his face. Barney opened his eyes and looked up, his mouth dropping open.

Pancho was silhouetted against the sun.

A crowd of bandits gathered behind their leader, encircling Barney.

"You wouldn't happen to be the — uh — Texas National Guard, would you?" Barney asked.

The look on the faces of the bandits answered Barney's question. He got a sinking feeling.

"Oh, shit."

"The river you crossed," Pancho said, "— it was the Rio Grande.

"Rio — Grande."

"You are now in Mexico, gringo."

"It's a — a lovely country. Really."

Pancho spat at Barney who put up his hands to shield his face. But it was a vinegaroon spider on the rock behind Barney that got splattered with well chewed tobacco.

Barney turned to see the varmint scoot away as the bandits laughed.

Barney got to his feet. He dusted himself off and extended his hand to Pancho.

"We haven't been introduced. I'm Barney Linedecker. Lt. Linedecker, U....S.....Army........"

Barney realized that he was saying the wrong thing. He let his unshaken hand fall back to his side and forced a smile to his face.

"I presume I'm speaking to Pancho -- the famous Pancho Villa."

Pancho's initial expression of joy at being recognized vanished in an instant.

"Villa? Villa????"

Barney knew he had done something else wrong, but he wasn't sure what?

Why everyone knows about Villa? What about me? What about Pancho Renteria? I have stolen more horses, more guns, robbed more banks, shot more soldiers -- and had more women than that dog Villa."

As if on cue, the bandits chimed in to support Pancho.

"Mucho!!! Mucho!!!"

Barney got to thinking that these clowns were crazy.

"Pancho Renteria is the true hero!" Pancho pronounced.

"Viva Pancho! Viva Pancho!!" his men cheered.

"I am the liberator of my people!"

He gestured to his men. They roared their approval.

"Why would that pig Villa get all the songs and stories written about him? I was stealing from peons and shooting gringos before he could even shave."

The bandits laughed.

"It is me they send the gringo Army to fight — my men they shoot — but Villa is all they write about."

"At least they didn't misspell your name."

Barney laughed — alone.

Pancho and his men started to close in on Barney. The young lieutenant had to think fast.

"Look, I'm on your side. They should be writing about you. Really."

Pancho stopped and so did his men.

"Maybe I can tell the newspapers some stories — real good stuff. Get them to do a whole issue on you."

Pancho liked this idea and thought it over. Then he laughed.

"I think I like you, Gringo. You make me laugh."

Pancho laughed again.

Then Pancho's smile faded.

"But we are not going to let you go, Gringo. You are my prisoner.

"Of course, I am. I never thought differently for a minute.

I was just thinking that -- well it's going to be hard to get the newspapers to do a story -- and do it correctly, unless I'm there to — uh — supply the details. See what I mean?"

Pancho took his hook and placed the tip end of it right under Barney's chin.

Barney's eyes were so wide that his eyeballs were apt to fall out at any moment. Barney got up on his tip toes.

"You make Pancho laugh. You are staying here, Gringo."

"Of course, I am. I sure am."

"They will write a story about me now — because I have a gringo soldier as a prisoner.

"Good point."

Instantly Barney wished he hadn't said that.

"I mean — about the prisoner. Villa certainly doesn't have any."

Pancho laughed again and let Barney down, pulling his hook away.

"I think I will have to burn your machine."

CHAPTER 8

Barney couldn't believe he was hearing correctly.

"Burn it? Say, you wouldn't kid about something like that would you?"

"Pancho Renteria does not joke about burning."

"I'm sorry. Of course, you don't."

"You want to try to stop us from burning it?"

"Not this gringo."

Pancho nodded in satisfaction. But Barney couldn't leave well enough alone.

"As a matter of fact, I'll even supply the matches."

Pancho's expression changed as Barney produced a box of wooden matches.

One of Pancho's lieutenants, Diego, leaned over to Pancho.

"Jefe. Why would he want us to burn his ma'chine?"

Pancho considered this. Barney took one match out of the box.

"If you'll open one of the fuel lines — pour some gasoline all over the sucker, it'll go up like — like a piece of trash. These things would rather burn than fly."

Pancho was no longer sure of his decision.

"You want to help us to burn your flyin' ma'shine? The only hope you have of escaping?"

"Escape? Who wants to escape? I'm no hero. I'm a prisoner. Look, if I escape, do you know what the Army would do? They'd put me right back in another one of those damn things — send me back up again. No, thank you. I'll stay down here with you — and make you laugh. Come on, let's make a real bonfire out of this piece of junk."

Pancho didn't know what to make of this. Even the bandit gang started to mumble about it.

"You, Gringo -- you *want* us to -- burn your ma'shine?"

"You got it. Here."

Barney offered the matches to Pancho. Pancho thought all of this over, not an easy process for him. Then he decided.

"Bring the gringo."

Pancho turned and headed for his horse.

Barney didn't like the way that sounded. A couple of bandits grabbed Barney as Diego got on his horse and Pancho mounted his.

"Jefe! What do we do with his ma'chine?"

"Bring it, too."

No one understood this order.

"Bring it, Jefe?"

"Bring it!"

Quickly Barney's hands were tied, and Diego selected a couple of bandits to get the plane. They didn't understand how to do the job. Barney picked up on this.

"Tell them — tell them they can push it by the wings. From the very end of the wings."

Pancho looked from Barney to the plane as the men crossed to the craft. Now Pancho was sure.

Laughing Pancho said, "Be very careful! Do not push it by the wings!"

Barney looked defeated.

The bandits moved out of the dry wash in a long line, Pancho in the lead, laughing as he went. Barney walked with a rope around his neck, his hands tied behind him. Diego led the group bringing the De Havilland. There were blankets around the tail section of the craft with ropes around the blanket which were, in turn, tied to saddle horns. They pulled the plane backwards.

⚜

HIGH UP IN THE BOULDERS, LYING ON HIS BELLY, A PAIR OF binoculars to his eyes, was Lurty. He was watching it all.

"A sure-as-hell pickle, by God. A sure-as-hell pickle," Lurty said.

He lowered the glasses after a moment and shook his head. Then Lurty eased his way back away from the edge.

⚜

THE ARMY CAMP WAS SETTLING DOWN FOR THE NIGHT. Guards were being posted. Lights, however, were on in the headquarters building.

Under the glow of a lamp, Col. Zane worked on a stack of paperwork at his desk. There was a knock at Zane's door.

"Come!" Col. Zane said.

Capt. Rendon entered with Staff Sgt. Orley Nester. Nester was such a slob that he made Rendon look very military indeed. He had something in his hand that he was eating a little at a time.

"Colonel, it's Sgt. Nester."

Nester saluted.

Zane's head began to pound with a migraine headache as soon as he heard Nester's name. Zane stood and crossed back to the window. He returned the salute with his back to the sergeant. He would have rather look into the dark than at the men before him. Zane rubbed his temple but did not turn.

"What is it, Sgt?"

Nester was nervous. He swallowed, rolled his eyes up in his head as a fart escaped his rear end. He was instantly embarrassed as Zane turned to glare at him.

"Sorry, Colonel." Nervously Nester popped something in his mouth to eat.

"What are you eating, Sgt?" Captain Rendon asked.

Nester opened his palm and showed Rendon. Nester had a very irritating voice.

"Beans, Sir."

"Beans?"

"Doc Starrett says they're good fer my heart. 'Course he says the more I eat the more I'll —

"I understand. Don't eat them in the Colonel's office."

"Oh. Of course, Sir." Nester shoved his handful of beans into his pants pocket.

Rendon tried to fan away the fragrance of Nester's emission.

"What is it, Sgt?" the Colonel asked.

"There's this rancher fella' outside, Sir. Says he's seen one of our planes go down."

Zane turned around interested but still in pain.

"Maybe it's Linedecker, Colonel."

"Get him in here, Sgt." Zane ordered.

CHAPTER 9

M oments later Sgt. Nester entered the Colonel's office with Lurty. Lurty was knocking trail dust off himself. He stopped right were Nester stood when he last spoke to Col. Zane. Lurty made a face.

"You boys ought t' bury whatever that is that died in here."

Nester hunched his shoulders sheepishly.

"Col. Zane, this is Mr. Lurty Ether — er —"

"Etheridge." Lurty said.

"Right."

Lurty reached across to Zane and offered his hand. Zane accepted it and the two men shook.

"Mr. Etheridge," Zane said.

"Lurty."

"Pardon?"

"Lurty. Said call me, Lurty. Ever'body does."

"Lurty," the Colonel said slowly.

Rendon stepped up and shook hands with Lurty.

"I'm Captain Rendon."

"Yeah, ain't you one of our Texas boys?"

"Yes, Sir. Texas National Guard. We've been nationalized to help deal with the bandit problem."

"Glad ever'body 'round here ain't a damn yankee."

Zane didn't like that, but his head hurt too much for him to care.

"Sgt. Nester tells me you saw one of our turkey — I mean — aeroplanes — go down."

"Bet ya' butt, I did."

There was a pause in which Zane expected Lurty to continue. It became obvious the rancher had no such intent.

"Would you mind telling us when — and where?"

"Nope. Don't mind a'tall."

Again Zane waited in vain for more information which didn't come.

"Well? Tell me."

"It was this afternoon. You starched britches is doin' such a bang up job, three Mes'cans was on my place tryin' t' rob me. That's when I first seen him."

"Exactly where is this?"

"Jest this side of Terlingua."

"That is where you saw our — machine?"

"Bet ya' butt. These three 'liberators' had th' drop on me. This — this flyin' thing come over. Scared th' pure-dee piss out of 'em. Damn Mes'cans thought th' sky was fallin'."

"Is that when the — pilot went down?

"Oh, hell, no. He done his job. Scared them bandits off and flew off himself."

"But you said you saw him go down?"

"Sure I did. But not then. That was later. See, after that I got th' drop on them Mes'cans an' run 'em off. But this fella flyin' that contraption looked t' me like he was havin' trouble. S' I decided t' foller 'im."

"And where did that lead you?"

"Cross th' river. Now that's where I seen it on th' ground."

"You mean the Rio Grande?" Rendon asked. "He crossed the border?"

"It ain't all that much of a border in lots of places. Hell, you can step on rocks some places -- get across without gettin' wet."

"Let me make sure I understand this. You're telling me this — pilot — put down in Mexico?"

"'Don't know if he intended to land there or if his machine quit on him. It was in a dry wash 'bout half a mile on th' other side. An' that ain't all."

"There's more?"

"He's been captured."

"By bandits?" Rendon asked.

Lurty nodded.

"They hauled him and his contraption off."

Zane's tone and his expression sounded as if he didn't believe Lurty's story.

"We appreciate the information, Mr. — Lurty."

"You don't believe me?"

Zane tried not to appear condescending but he couldn't help it.

"No one said that. We will check into this."

"Sure you will. Th' day fat pigs fly."

"Sgt., show Mr. -- the gentleman the way out." Then to Lurty Zane added, "If one of our men is over there, we'll find him."

"Shit, you starched britches can't find your bare butt with both hands if ya' had a map."

Lurty walked out and Sgt. Nester went with him.

"Sir." Rendon said after he closed the door, "I don't understand. You think he's making this all up?"

"I don't know what he's doing, Captain. It could be a case of protracted sunstroke."

"But, Sir. An eyewitness report?"

Zane crossed to a map on his wall.

"I have the latest intelligence from General Pershing's G-2. Pancho Villa is in the hills across from Vera Cruz. There is no way he could get from there to near Terlingua in one day."

"Yes, Sir."

"You have to be careful of information from local inhabitants. They see things in a much different way than the Army does. But to be on the safe side, find out what you can about Mr. — Lurty."

CHAPTER 10

"I already know a little, Sir." Capt. Rendon said after Sgt. Nester and Lurty had gone out the front door of the building. "He is a big rancher around here. Remember that patrol we sent out last week?"

"What about it?"

"That was the patrol that fell apart when they came up on that young woman taking a bath in a stock pond."

"The young woman with the — *gargantuan* endowments?"

"That's the one, Sir. Seems she stood up and waved at the patrol."

"There you have it. Any father who can't teach his daughter any better — manners — than that —.

"She was being friendly."

"Captain. We are not going to put much stock in tales told by a father like that."

"Yes, Sir."

Zane crossed back to his window.

"There's an honest to God war going on in Europe. A real war."

"We all know, Sir."

"That's where I should be — fighting the Kaiser. Not out here chasing wetbacks and A.W.O.L. turkey buzzards."

"So, what do we do about Linedecker? I mean, assuming there's even a thread of truth in — Lurty's report?"

Zane sighed. He had the weight of the world on him.

"I suppose we'll have to take a patrol out."

"In the morning?"

"Daybreak."

"Shall I assign Lt. Jerrald?"

"No. We are going to do this one, Captain."

Rendon didn't like what he was hearing.

"We, Sir? As in -- you and me?"

"You can ride a horse, can't you, Captain?"

"Yes, Sir, but —"

"Daybreak, Captain."

Rendon saw that it was hopeless. He resigned himself to it.

"Yes, Sir."

Rendon saluted and exited.

"Automobiles — aeroplanes — National Guard — women voting. This whole country is going right down the crapper," Col. Zane muttered to himself in disgust.

WHAT DROPPED ONTO A TIN PLATE LOOKED LIKE IT CAME from a crapper. Barney, his hands no longer tied, was holding the plate as he stood at the end of a chow line amid crumbling adobe buildings. This was once a town but now served as the bandit's hideout.

Somewhere nearby a man screamed. Barney looked up startled. The bandits around the camp fires laughed.

Another spoonful of the unidentified matter was slopped onto Barney's plate. He jerked it away before they gave him more. He stepped away. A guard carrying a rifle followed him.

In the light of the campfires other guards were standing watch on the tops of the buildings. Another scream was heard followed by more laughter from the bandits.

A kissing sound was heard. Barney turned and saw Carmella.

She looked like a Spanish escapee from a Verdi opera. If she sang, it would be all over. She was puckered up and blowing kisses at Barney.

Barney was horrified at the thought. He quickly stepped away through groups of bandits and assorted other women. Barney was looking for a place to sit but wasn't sure where a good place might be.

"Over here!" a male voice called out.

Barney looked in the direction of the voice. He discovered an American in his 50's (or early 90's – it was hard to tell). He was dressed in dark pants and a dark vest over a yellowing white shirt. He was drying his hands on a cloth outside one of the buildings. A bandit came out of the building behind the older man. The bandit was holding his crouch and sneering at the American.

The older man motioned to Barney.

"Young man. Join me over here."

Barney crossed and entered the open door frame. The man extended his hand to Barney.

"Lyndon P. Starrett. Folks call me, Doc," the man said.

"Doctor?" Barney asked.

"What passes for one for a couple hundred miles in any direction."

"Barney Linedecker," Barney said shaking hands

"An officer, right?"

"Yes. But also the lowest form of life in the Army."

"My God, they' captured a general?"

"Hardly. I'm a Lt. A 2nd Lt."

"Still, an officer and a gentleman — by act of Congress."

Barney frowned and sat with his plate.

"Not in my case."

"How's that?"

"It's a long story."

"An act of God couldn't make a gentlemen of me, son!"

If appearances were any measure of Starrett, then Barney would have to agree.

"But you're a doctor."

"I didn't finish medical school. The dean wanted me to marry his daughter simply because we had slept together a few times. I didn't cotton to the idea and neither did she."

Barney turned his attention to his plate.

"This stuff safe to eat?"

"Sure. And it's fresh."

Barney took a bite.

"It doesn't taste too bad, either, does it?" Doc Starrett said. "Refried beans — and coyote. Saw 'em shoot it myself. You'll find it not s' hard in these parts to develop a taste for coyote tamales."

CHAPTER 11

Barney choked on his coyote and beans. He forced the meat out of his mouth.

"Coyote?"

"Yeah. It was a good, healthy bitch. And beans.

Barney put his plate down. Starrett shrugged and picked it up.

"You sure you don't want it?"

"Be my guest," Barney said as he waved it away.

Starrett chowed down with gusto.

"I've got a theory. See, I've got hemorrhoids -- bad, sometimes. An ol' prospector told me that boiled coyote is the best thing in the world for it. Ya' never saw a prairie wolf with hemorrhoids, did ya'?"

Starrett continued to eat and Barney had to turn away. Just the idea of coyote was too much for him.

Right about then Carmella and one of the bandits walked by. Carmella was prissing and made a point of giving a big bump in Barney's direction as she passed.

The doctor noticed.

"Looks like you've got yourself an admirer, there."

"Just what I need — the Battleship Maine — in a skirt."

"I'd be careful there, son. She could be a lot of help t' you."

"Her?"

"She's Pancho's little sister."

"Does he have a *big* sister?

"Take some advice, though. Don't go playing Roll-Me-Over-In-The-Clover with her."

"I'd have to be out of my mind."

"You might be surprised. Carmella is rather — persuasive. Fact is, she's th' reason I'm here."

Barney turned to Starrett. Then he cut his eyes back to Carmella who disappeared behind a wall with one of the bandits. Barney looked back to Starrett.

"I know there are men who like women who are —

He gestures with his hands spread apart. Barney didn't know how to say "enormous" in a nice way.

"Oh, no," Doc Starrett said. "That's not it. Well, not usually, anyway. For these men it's a case of supply and demand. Carmella had the supply — an endless supply it would appear. And inspite of everything, some of these men have such a demand — well things happen."

"You're an American, aren't you?" Barney asked.

"Yes. But I live over here. Well, not right here — but on this side of th' river. Of course, I have patients on both sides. Pancho gets me t' drop in ever' s' often."

Starrett wiped his mouth on the back of his sleeve.

"You might say I'm a regular guest. I come t' treat Pancho's men. Ever'thing from bug bites t' gunshots t' — the clap. Mostly the clap."

Barney looked after Carmella with a different expression.

"That's right. Carmella is th' main carrier. And these men know it."

Barney shook with a shiver of revulsion at the very thought of going to bed with Carmella. Back to Starrett he said, "That's what all the screaming was about?"

"The ol' red hot needle up the diseased organ. It's still the only cure."

Barney grabbed his crotch.

"You treat her, too, don't you?"

"Oh, no."

"Why not?"

"My life isn't much -- but I'm kind a' partial to it."

Barney didn't get it.

"Pancho doesn't like the thought of his — *little sister* — being anything but a virgin."

" A virgin?"

Starrett hushed Barney.

"You want a hook right in your gizzard?"

Barney understood. He stood and moved a couple of steps.

The Guard narrowed his eyes at Barney.

Barney turned and looked over toward his plane which sat at the edge of camp. The craft was guarded by a couple of bandits. Starrett put the plate down and took out a pipe which he filled and lit.

"Doctor Starrett —"

"Just Doc. Two and a half years at Johns Hopkins -- best damn medical school in th' country. But, like I said, no degree or diploma. Round these parts, everyone calls me Doc. What about yourself?"

Barney was angry with himself just thinking about his predicament.

"Let's just say I'm Mr. Pancho's guest — uninvited — "

"Well, hell, I can see that."

" — but not a totally unwilling guest," Barney added.

"Young fella', I don't think you understand the kind of fix you could be in. Pancho Gancho isn't anyone's idea of a nice man."

Barney stretched as if he were ready to go to bed.

"Oh, I don't know. He seems okay to me."

"You might want to start thinkin' about escapin'."

"Escaping? Me? No, thank you."

Starrett started to say something when a commotion erupted with approaching horses. There were "whoops" from the riders.

"What's going on?"

"I've got no idea."

CHAPTER 12

E miliano, Martin, and Beto were the bandits who rode up. Martin and Beto dismounted to the shouting and whistling of the other bandits.

Emiliano swung a leg over his saddle horn and slipped out of the saddle. As he did, he revealed someone on his horse behind him.

It was Addie. Her hands were tied behind her, making the best display of her most obvious assets.

The expression on Addie's face changed from fear to expectation, to sultry aloofness and then back to little girl in fear again.

Pancho stepped forward through the crowd.

"Silencio! Silencio!!"

He stopped in his tracks when he saw Addie. He nodded his approval. Emiliano, Martin, and Beto were all grins at their success.

Pancho pulled the girl down and circled her approvingly.

At Pancho's smile several bandits fired off rounds and shouted.

Pancho stepped over to Emiliano, Martin, and Beto. In Spanish the three told their tale.

Addie was forgotten by Pancho for the moment, and she became the center of attention for all the other bandits. They looked her over and make suggestive gestures.

She wondered if this is the "fate worse than death" she had been warned about.

But as she surveyed her soon-to-be-attackers, she saw something else. She looked again and then broke into a dead run.

Addie raced past Pancho and all the other bandits. She ran straight to Barney and Doc Starrett.

She dropped to her knees in front of Barney who didn't know what to do or think. He glanced at Starrett who backed away as if to say "Don't look at me."

"You're safe!!!" Addie crooned.

Barney didn't understand.

"Yes," he said hesitantly.

Pancho and the rest of the bandit kingdom gathered around.

"I was so worried," Addie said.

She nuzzled Barney's leg.

Again he didn't know what to do or say.

"Ah — wait. Are you the girl in the stock pond?"

Addie lit up.

"You did see me!"

Pancho strode right up to Barney and Addie.

Barney forced an innocent smile.

"The Gringo flyer has a senorita," Pancho said.

The crowd laughed.

"I — uh — I don't know this — girl. I've seen her — all of her in fact — but —"

Addie nuzzled Barney's leg once more.

"I think she knows you, Señor. Or wants to."

The crowd laughed.

Addie looked up at Barney.

"Don't let them touch me. Please!"

Barney couldn't believe he was hearing this. How the hell could he protect her? He was sure the girl was nuts.

"Are you going to fight us for her, Gringo?"

"Fight?"

Barney swallowed and tried to smile but it wouldn't come.

The bandits all suddenly looked very mean. Barney tried to back away from Addie, but she clung to him. Pancho laughed.

"Look — isn't there some other way we can work this out?" Barney pleaded.

Pancho motioned Emiliano, Martin, and Beto forward.

"Some of my best men have gone to a lot of trouble to pick this little flower for us."

"I'm sure they do very good work," Barney said grinning.

Pancho laughed and said, "But now she wants *you*, Gringo. And they -- they want her."

Pancho drew his knife. The crowd cheered.

"I think somebody will have to get cut up — a little," Pancho grinned.

The crowd loved this and Pancho laughed at his own joke.

"Bring torches!"

Some of the bandits stepped away and then returned with flaming torches which lit up the area.

Barney looked around for help. Doc Starrett slunk away. Barney realized he was screwed.

Pancho crossed to Barney and Addie. He flipped a big knife in his hand. He stopped right in front of the pair and offered the weapon to Barney. Pancho gestured for some of the other bandits to move Addie away. They did.

Pancho still held the knife but Barney made no move to take it. Pancho poked Barney in the stomach with the butt of the blade. Barney reached to protect his middle and caught the knife in his right hand as Pancho released it.

Pancho stepped back as the bandits formed a large circle.

Emiliano stepped forward drawing his knife and tossing off his sombrero.

Pancho motioned to Beto who stepped forward with an inch thick, long piece of leather.

Emiliano extended his left hand and Pancho tied one end of the strap to it. Pancho then turned, with the other end, to Barney.

"Which is your fighting hand, Gringo?"

"Fighting hand? I don't have one."

Pancho translated for the crowd which burst into laughter.

Pancho reached for Barney's left hand. He lashed the free end of the leather strap to Barney's left wrist.

Emiliano was enjoying this spectacle greatly.

Addie and Starrett watched from the crowd.

CHAPTER 13

Doc Starrett spoke to Addie who was watching not really understanding what was going on.

"What were you doing away from the ranch?" he asked.

Addie pointed at Barney, "Lookin' for him."

Starrett looked at Barney then back at Addie.

"Why?"

"I think I'm in love, Doc. I've never felt this way before."

"Honey, that's not love."

"I don't care. Doc, I don't want to be an old maid. If I don't get away from Daddy, that's what I'll be. The only way I'll ever get away from Daddy is by getting married. And the *only* way I'll ever get married is if I have to."

The two turned back to the fight.

When he was finished tying the two men together, Pancho stepped back. He signaled by dropping one arm in a quick motion — and the fight was on.

Emiliano wrapped some of the strap around his hand and tugged a couple of times to get the feel of Barney.

Barney was jerked with each pull and stumbled a few steps.

Then Barney caught on and tried to wrap some of the leather around his hand. But before he could, Emiliano yanked hard, sending Barney stumbling again. Barney staggered until Emiliano stuck his leg out and tripped Barney, forcing him face down in the sand. The young pilot got a good mouth full of earth.

Barney came up spitting and coughing. Emiliano and the others all roared with laughter.

Barney took a deep breath and climbed to his feet. He wrapped the leather around his hand and gave Emiliano a yank — only the tactic backfired. Emiliano also yanked, but the Mexican yanked harder.

Emiliano caught Barney and shoved him back to the ground. All this was to another round of laughter.

Emiliano now got serious about the fight. He took a couple of steps forward and waited while Barney climbed back to his feet. Once more Pancho signaled for the fight to continue.

Emiliano took a couple of swipes at Barney who managed to avoid each pass only by inches or hairs. Emiliano slung Barney around by the leather strap and tried to cut Barney in as many ways as he could.

Barney was so busy keeping out of harm's way that he made no offensive moves.

Emiliano jerked Barney off his feet and tried to slice him across the back as Barney rolled over and over.

Barney even crawled to get out of Emiliano's way.

Once on his feet again, Barney all but ran to keep away from Emiliano's blade.

This was a very one-sided fight. Suddenly there was a swipe by Emiliano and clothes ripped.

There was a gasp from the crowd and Barney opened his eyes wide in horror.

He froze and then forced himself to look down.

There, parallel to the fly of his pants, was a gaping hole, sliced clean through. The white of his underwear showed.

Emiliano looked at his work and erupted into laughter which was echoed by the crowd.

Addie gasped as Barney looked up angry.

This had gone far enough. Barney wrapped the leather strap around his wrist and with both hands he yanked.

Emiliano was jerked out of his laughter as Barney snapped the strap.

This got both Emiliano's ire up and the crowds' attention. Emiliano crouched, spat and began circling Barney.

Barney stooped over and was in a fighting posture, too.

Emiliano yanked Barney with the strap and Barney dug both heels in and returned the favor.

Barney's jerk of the strap surprised Emiliano and almost caused him to fall. The Mexican got angry and moved to snap the cord, but Barney cut the leather just as Emiliano pulled. The bandit flew backward through the crowd before he hit the ground. He landed on a cactus and screamed as Pancho led the crowd laughing.

Emiliano got up and was about to charge Barney when Pancho stepped forward again.

Pancho picked up the ends of the strap and retied them, laughing all the time. Pancho also pulled out his pistol.

Still laughing, Pancho said, "If you cut the rope again, Gringo, — I will have to kill you."

Pancho stepped back away and Emiliano yanked Barney.

The two men circled each other. Emiliano got hold of the strap and began slinging Barney around and around.

Barney started to get air sick.

Emiliano jumped toward Barney slashing as he moved. This caused the Lt. to fall to the ground.

Emiliano leapt over and slashed at Barney who rolled and twisted to miss the bandit's blade.

Barney even crawled through Emiliano's legs and flipped Emiliano over with the strap. But in the process Barney dropped Pancho's knife. Before he could get hold of it again, Emiliano was slashing at him. Barney had to scurry away on his hands and knees.

The crowd loved this comedy — Barney crawling, Emiliano chasing him. The bandit was getting more and more angry with each missed attack.

Finally Emiliano moved around and kicked sand in Barney's face.

Barney couldn't see a thing. He was down on all fours fighting to get the sand out of his eyes. Emiliano stepped forward and raised his blade high over his head for the final plunge into Barney.

CHAPTER 14

Barney, still on his knees in the sand, had located Pancho's knife and held it with both hands. The tip of the blade was right in Emiliano's crotch.

Emiliano froze. He swallowed but didn't move another muscle. Pancho stepped over to the pair. He was surprised.

"It looks like the Gringo wins!"

Barney didn't move and neither did Emiliano.

"But — if you win — you will have to then fight Emiliano's friends. I don't think you can beat them all."

The crowd pressed forward with some really mean looking bandits at the forefront.

"I will tell you what, Gringo. We will make a deal."

"I'm listening," Barney said not really sure all of this was going to end well.

"Let's say you won the senorita," Pancho smiled.

"What's the rest of it?

"If you want to keep her — and not have to fight all of Emiliano's friends — you will have to give *us* something.

"What? What have I got?"

"You could let Emilino keep his cahones — and you could give *me* your flyin' m'chine."

"That's it? That's all you want?"

Pancho nodded and laughed.

Addie waited breathlessly.

Barney still held Emiliano in position. Something about Pancho's offer didn't add up.

"But — you already have the plane."

Pancho leaned over and spoke quietly to Barney.

"Gringo. If Pancho doesn't get something out of this deal — you get your throat cut. Now you make up your mind."

Pancho stood up again. Barney didn't have to think this over very long. But he did motion to Emiliano's knife.

"He drops his knife first."

Pancho nodded. Pancho looked over at Emiliano as a signal.

Emiliano released his blade. It stabbed into the ground a few inches away from Barney.

Barney lowered his knife and pulled back. Emiliano came down off his tiptoes.

Barney then stood and returned Pancho's knife. Pancho took the weapon and put it back in his scabbard. Then he spoke to Emiliano in Spanish. Next Pancho turned to Barney.

"Shake hands. You are amigos now."

Emiliano extended his hand, Barney took it and they shook. Pancho turned and spoke to the crowd in Spanish. When Pancho finished, there was a cheer from the crowd.

Addie was released and she ran to Barney.

Doc Starrett crossed to Barney and Addie.

"Ya' did all right, young fella'."

"Thanks for the help!"

"I've stayed alive a lot of years out here, son. Done it by mindin' my own business."

Barney noticed that Addie was looking at the slit in his trousers. He covered it with his hands and turned away from her.

Doc laughed.

Pancho turned back to Barney, Addie, and Doc as the bandit crowd broke up and got about their business.

"Well, Gringo — I give you a room."

Barney was on guard. What did that mean? Pancho laughed.

"For you and your senorita."

Addie smiled with expectation.

Pancho slapped Barney on the back.

"I will see you in the morning."

Pancho pointed at the sky, nodded and then walked off.

"I want to see that, too," Doc Starrett said.

"See what?"

"I forgot. You don't know the lingo. Pancho says you will give him your flying buggy there."

"He's welcome to it."

"He also said," Addie added, "you're gonna take him for a ride — in th' mornin'."

"A what?"

Barney broke out in a cold sweat of complete horror.

A WHILE LATER ADDIE SAT AGAINST AN ADOBE WALL OF A shack threading a needle.

"What's s' bad about that? It's just a little ride. I'd like that, too."

"It means flying. Have you ever flown?"

"Of course not. But it sounds like fun."

From behind another partially crumbling wall, Barney stepped out of his trousers and handed them to Addie — over the wall.

"Well, take my word for it. It is *not* fun. Dangerous — stupid — insane. But it definitely is not fun!"

Addie spread Barney's pants out on her lap. She stroked the cloth where it was cut and sighed. Then she licked her lips as she unbuttoned the fly, getting more and more excited as she did.

CHAPTER 15

From behind the broken down adobe wall, Barney talked while Addie sewed on his pants.

"Do you have any idea what we call those things?"

Addie was still looking at Barney's pants.

"You have a name for it?"

"We call 'em flaming coffins."

"Daddy calls his Little Lurty."

Barney looked over at Addie. He wasn't sure they were even talking about the same thing. He shook his head and went on. He made sure he was standing behind the half crumbled wall keeping the lower half of his body out of Addie's line of sight.

"Flaming coffins! They'll catch fire — crash — flip over -- crack up — explode!! They do anything better than they fly."

Barney shook his head as he said, "If God had wanted man to fly — he wouldn't have invented the railroad."

Barney realized he had stepped out from behind the wall,

and Addie was looking at his legs and underwear. He stepped back.

"Would you please fix my pants?"

Addie giggled and went back to sewing.

"You don't really need them fixed — not tonight."

"I most certainly do."

"Not for me."

"What is that supposed to mean?"

She tried to act coy, but the act didn't really work.

"We don't know if we'll come back from here alive. Don't you think we ought t' make th' most of every moment we have? It's not as if you ain't earned th' right. You did fight for me."

"Look, Miss —. What is your name?"

"Addie. Addie Etheridge."

"Miss Etheridge — we had better —"

"I wish you'd call me Addie."

"Add — Miss Etheridge —"

"And what's your name?"

"Oh, uh — Linedecker. Lt. Barney Linedecker."

Addie mused over Barney's name.

"Linedecker. That has a nice sound to it. Lt. and Mrs. Linedecker."

Barney didn't like the sound of their conversation. Then suddenly he was saved by a knock at the door.

"Come in," Barney said.

Doc Starrett entered with a big grin on his face.

"Hope I'm not interrupting anything — yet."

Disappointedly Addie said, "No, Doc. You're not."

To the doctor Barney said, "Did you talk to him?"

"Pancho's mind's made up. Tomorrow morning. You and Pancho and the flyin' buggy. It's an appointment with destiny."

"More like an appointment with a mortician."

Barney stepped out from behind the wall. He then realized once again his state of undress and retreated.

The doctor sat and scratched his head.

"Would you mind tellin' me what this problem is with you and flyin'?"

Addie leaned over and whispered to Doc, "I'd like to know about his problem with women."

Barney looked out a hole in the wall where a window used to be and shook his head. Some privacy, he thought.

"Me and flying. That involves the three dumbest things I've done in my life."

"Sounds like you have a problem, there."

Barney turned back to Starrett and Addie.

"You have to understand my family. The Linedeckers have been military heroes all the way back to — I don't know — Attila the Hun, I guess. Fighting is supposed to be in our blood. The only thing in my blood is chicken pox. Take my grandfather — now there's a fruitcake — with too much rum in it. He loved to play soldier. In the Civil War he fought on both sides — at different times. He didn't care as long as he was fighting. My father ran off to play cavalry in Cuba. He was shot in the rear at San Juan Hill — he claims by Teddy Roosevelt! Roosevelt fell off his horse and his pistol went off. Dad got a purple heart — for getting lead in his butt."

Starrett and Addie exchanged glances and smiles.

"Everybody in my family has been a hero. And it's made a lot of money — being on the board of directors of banks, companies — that kind of thing. Now it's my turn. In order to inherit the family money, I have to 'earn' the family name. I'm supposed to 'distinguish myself in the military service of my country.' Well, I thought I'd just go down and join up and do my duty — I mean, we're not at war with anyone right now. The second dumbest thing I ever did. The first was being born into this deranged family. As soon as I got to boot camp, I knew I could kiss that money good-bye."

Addie put Barney's pants to her mouth to bite off the thread. She tossed Barney's pants to him. He caught them and examined her work.

The stitches were neither neat nor particularly secure.

Sarcastically he said, "You do beautiful work."

"My heart wasn't in it." Then with a wink to Doc she says, "I ain't even had a chance t' practice what I think I'll be best at."

Addie smiled, but Barney frowned at this. He stepped into his pants. Addie got up and handed the needle to Doc.

"Thanks for the loan of the needle, Doc."

"Glad I could help."

She winked at Doc.

CHAPTER 16

"Don't put too much strain on that tear," Addie said. "It just might not hold. And out you'd pop."

Barney emerged from behind the broken down wall wearing his pants.

"I'll be extra careful."

To Doc Starrett Addie said disappointedly, "That's what I'm afraid of."

Barney crossed to Doc. Doc lit up his pipe.

"And you've made up your mind — you're not going to be brave — no matter what?"

"Brave is just another word for either stupid or crazy. Heroes. They take chances no rational, sane person would. They put themselves in dangerous situations — intentionally. I'd rather be a live coward than a dead hero."

"I've always thought heroes were cowards who got backed into a corner. They did what they had to do," Doc said.

"Not this coward. You back me in a corner and I'll crawl out the back door."

"Like you did in that knife fight?"

"That was a brave thing you did," Addie said.

"No, that was stupid."

"And a little crazy?" Doc asked.

"I was only trying to save myself."

"It was still brave," Addie said admiringly.

"Remember Nathan Hale?" Doc asked, "'I regret I have but one life to give for my country.'"

"If he had another one, he could have been hung twice."

"And Davy Crockett — and Jim Bowie," Addie added.

"Have you noticed -- all those guys are dead?"

"But they still write stories, and poems, and songs about them," Doc said taking a draw from his pipe.

"I don't see anyone writing anything about me."

"Then let's try." Doc offered. He thought a moment.

"There was a young pilot Linedecker — who hated flying —"

Addie tried to help. "

--- and --- and checkers."

"Caught in Ol' Mexico — by a bandit named Pancho," Doc continued. "In a knife fight — 'near lost his pecker."

Barney wasn't impressed.

Addie got the drift of this and started the next verse.

"Saved a damsel named Addie —

Doc picked it up, "— from all of those Mexican --- baddies."

"She thinks he's a hero."

Barney added the next line. "But he knows he's a zero."

Doc finished the verse, "Might end up with Carmella the fattie."

Addie clapped at this.

Barney realized he'd better get control of the poem before it got out of hand. He started the next verse.

"He died young on the Mexican border; Listening to a doctor who wasn't quite sober. He could have lived long; but instead there's this song: about Barney who's no wiser or older."

❧

THE NEXT MORNING THE DE HAVILLAND HAD BEEN MOVED out to a stretch of flatland. Bandits stood around, laid around or remained on horseback in view of the plane. Pancho was talking to Emiliano and Diego.

The three Americans stood near the plane.

Barney asked Doc, "Couldn't you make him understand?"

"Believe me, son, I tried."

"Did you tell him I *won't* fly!"

Suddenly a pistol was jammed on the end of Barney's nose. Barney's eyes opened as wide as possible — then they crossed as he studied the weapon. He swallowed hard as an audible click announced the pistol was cocked.

"However, I do reserve the right to change my mind. I just did."

It was Pancho who held the pistol to Barney's nose. He laughed at Barney's remark.

Pancho lowered the pistol but grabbed Barney's pants with his hook between the young flyer's legs. He pulled Barney closer.

"You teach me how to fly this plane — or you won't be able to walk or crawl anymore."

"I believe we've reached a common ground of understanding." Barney said.

Pancho laughed and let Barney go.

Pancho climbed into the rear cockpit. He traded his sombrero for a pair of goggles on the seat. He turned and waved to his men.

The bandits laughed approvingly and fired weapons in the air yelling.

Barney was trying his best to be a good soldier — or airman. He leaned into the cockpit to instruct Pancho.

"This is the switch. This way is off — " he flipped the switch, "this way is on. It has to be on to start the motor."

"Switch," Pancho confirmed.

"The throttle here determines how fast the engine will go. You pull it out to increase the RPM's and you push it in to —
"

Pancho asked, "R - P - N's?"

"RPM's. Revolutions Per Minute."

Pancho said loudly, "There is only one revolution. And Pancho is the leader."

The bandits again shot off their guns into the air.

"Ah — let me try again. Pull this out to go faster — push it in to slow down."

Bucking his hips the bandit leader said, "Pancho's in and out always goes faster."

The bandits laughed at the joke.

Barney rolled his eyes. He reached down between Pancho's legs and grabbed the stick.

"This is 'the stick' — the joy stick."

Pancho made an obscene gesture with it. He described the joy stick to his followers in Spanish.

The bandit gang laughed.

Barney tried to struggle on, "It controls the elevators on the tail —," Barney pointed to the tail of the plane as he moved the stick. "— which decides if you go right or left — up or down. Forward is down. Back is up."

He pointed to the ailerons which move. Barney looked around for something — anything to show Pancho.

"Oh, yes. The pedals."

"They control the ailerons on the wings" He demonstrated.

Next he pointed to the gas cap between the two cockpits.

"This is the gas tank." Barney had an idea. "There may not be enough gas."

He looked at the gas gauge on the dashboard. It was about half full.

Barney frowned.

"Now, I am ready to fly," Pancho announced.

"I'm not."

Pancho's pistol came out again and attached itself to Barney's nose.

"Now I'm ready."

CHAPTER 17

"First, we'll have to start the motor," Barney said to Pancho. "It doesn't always want to start."

Pancho produced his pistol again saying, "You will make sure it starts now."

"Of course, I will," Barney said with a swallow. He walked around to the front of the plane.

Barney grabbed the propeller and pushed it around so he could get a good hold of it.

To Pancho he said, "Turn the switch — off."

Pancho had to locate the switch. He found it and flipped it off.

"All right, Gringo. The switch is off."

Barney spun the prop half way around and then repeated the process.

"This gets a little fuel in the carb. The motor."

Pancho smiled and waved to his men who responded.

Barney shook his head. He couldn't believe this stupidity. But he had to continue with it.

"Now, switch on."

Pancho flipped the switch and grinned at Barney.

Barney spun the prop and the motor caught the first time. It scared the hell out of him. This had never happened before. Barney hit the dirt and had to crawl under the plane — fast — to get beside Pancho. Barney made it to the cockpit, reached in and shut the throttle down to a tolerable range.

Pancho was pleased.

The bandits' horses shied away, and the bandits were trying to keep them in check.

Barney stepped back away from the plane as Pancho played with the other controls. The pilot was content to watch Pancho play with the joy stick and the pedals. But Pancho noticed Barney just standing there. The bandit leader shook his head and pulled out his pistol once more.

Barney sighed and resigned himself. He climbed into the front cockpit. He put on his cap and goggles. Pancho followed Barney's example.

He revered the motor and maneuvered the craft around. Then Barney pulled back on the throttle and the plane rolled down the flats gathering speed.

Pancho was experiencing pure glee.

Barney was already showing signs of nausea. He pulled back on the joy stick.

The plane rose in the air.

The bandits on the ground cheered.

As Barney prayed, Pancho enjoyed the new experience. He looked back at the shrinking landscape.

The De Havilland flew on up in the morning sky.

Barney was getting seriously ill by now. He started to sway in the cockpit. He turned to Pancho.

Pancho had his pistol out again and aimed at Barney.

Barney cupped his hand over his mouth to hold it back, but it looked as if that wouldn't be enough. Pancho pulled the hammer back on the pistol. The revolver had an amazing healing effect over Barney. He forced himself to swallow.

Barney's urge to throw up passed and he slumped back in his cockpit. He looked to heaven for an answer as to why all of this was happening to him.

The De Havilland flew on.

THE SOLDIERS OF C TROOP WERE MOUNTED AND FOLLOWED Lt. Col. Zane, Capt. Rendon and Sgt. Nester away from camp.

Col. Zane was not happy — but then no one under his command had ever seen him when he was.

Capt. Rendon did seem to enjoy what he was doing — but then he was only playing at being a mounted cavalry soldier.

Dust rose behind the troops as they headed out and started along their way.

Sgt. Nester lifted his bulk up in his saddle, strained, and then sat back down. The two soldiers behind him looked sick.

"I always thought if we got gassed — it would be by the enemy," the first said.

The second replied, "What makes you think he's on our side?"

AS BARNEY AND PANCHO FLEW ALONG, UNKNOWINGLY they were headed toward the troops. Pancho looked over the side of the cockpit and was enjoying the ride.

Barney was not sick at the moment but was flying without

being aware of what he was doing. It was all on automatic. He was trying to think of a way out of this mess. But everything that came to mind, he discarded with a shake of his head and a frown. He looked again to heaven. His expression became more and more plaintive — why him?

Suddenly the plane weaved and started to climb. Barney sat up and looked down at the joy stick. He was having to fight to control it, and he was losing.

The De Havilland dipped and bobbed in the air, swerving from side to side.

Barney studied the joy stick — he even let go of it, keeping his hands cupped a few inches away from it.

The joy stick moved by itself.

Barney looked down in the cockpit and followed the cables from the joy stick toward the rear of the plane.

The second joy stick, the one in the other cockpit, was being operated by Pancho!

CHAPTER 18

B arney felt the sudden need for more fervent prayer and divine intervention. Then he quickly looked back at Pancho.

Pancho's gun hand was still filled with the pistol. And it was still aimed at Barney.

Barney turned back around in his seat, checked to make sure his seat belt was fastened as tightly as it would go. Then he grabbed onto the sides of the cockpit with both hands, and closed his eyes. He didn't even want to see what was about to happen.

Pancho was truly in hog heaven. He pulled the throttle out all the way and pulled back on the joy stick.

The De Havilland climbed. It climbed higher and higher — going through clouds and going on up. Finally it had climbed as high as it would go. It stalled.

Pancho didn't understand what was happening. He pulled back on the joy stick even harder, but it didn't help. He looked around as the plane started to fall — backwards.

The De Havilland dropped from its stall, backwards at first and then it went into a nose dive.

Barney was biting his lip and pressing his eyes closed with all his strength. Somehow he hoped this would make the impact of hitting the ground a little more tolerable.

Pancho was in a panic. He didn't know what to do. He let go of the joy stick.

Pancho's eyes flashed with fear. His face broke out in a sweat as the plane continued to dive.

The ground rushed toward the plane. Clouds whizzed past the craft.

The joy stick in Barney's cockpit was free. It struck him in the leg as the craft whirled in a twisting dive.

Barney opened his eyes and saw the ground rushing toward them. He slammed his eyes closed again. Then he managed to squint through one eye at the joy stick. He opened his other eye.

Barney finally reached for the stick with both hands.

⚜

THE CAVALRY CONTINUED ON ITS WAY. ONE OF THE soldiers looked up. His expression was one of shock. He slapped the soldier beside him. They both looked up.

Something caused Capt. Rendon to look up. He dropped his mouth open.

Rendon shouted, "Colonel!"

Zane was of course irritated. "What, Capt.?"

The Colonel turned to Rendon and then followed his junior officer's eyes skyward.

"Isn't that one of ours?" Zane inquired.

"Unless the Mexicans have an airport."

Sgt. Nester moved forward.

"Sir, it's going to crash! On us!"

The De Havilland was spinning in its dive.

Pancho was now praying, too. He was willing to do anything to keep from dying.

Barney had already decided to do something. His hands grasped the joy stick and firmly tried to move it to the right.

The De Havilland slowed its spin and finally stopped spinning all together. But it continued to dive.

Pancho opened his eyes. It was a miracle! He looked at his pistol in his hand. He resolved to keep the promise he made in his prayer. He threw his pistol out of the plane.

The weapon flew through the air and hit one of the guide-wires holding the wings together. The pistol discharged.

The soldiers below kept watch on the diving airplane.

"He firing on us!" Col. Zane shouted. "Scatter!!"

The soldiers dove off their horses and tried to take cover or they spurred their horses away from the area.

Barney leaned back in the cockpit as he then pulled back on the joy stick.

The craft swooped down but came out of the dive — but in doing so it buzzed the troop column. Somehow it actually started to climb again.

Soldiers were holding their heads and praying as the plane flashed by. Some horses bolted. Some of the troops who were still on their mounts were thrown to the ground by the frightened animals.

Col. Zane was one of those thrown from his mount.

Capt. Rendon tried to bury his head in the dirt — the hell with his horse.

Sgt. Nester held his horse firmly from his hiding place

behind a boulder. As the plane zipped by, Nester looked around and felt rather superior. He smirked as he stepped out.

To Col. Zane, the sergeant said, "Need some help — Sir?"

The Colonel looked up angrily at Nester.

Rendon searched the skies for the plane.

"It's number 13, Sir," Rendon said. "It has to be Lt. Linedecker."

Zane's frown deepened at that thought.

"What in the hell is he trying to kill us for?"

"Sir?" Rendon asked.

Pancho's pistol struck the ground and discharged again. The round ricocheted a couple of times off the rocks near the soldiers.

CHAPTER 19

S uddenly Nester decided that the better part of valor was in retreat. He dove for cover.

Col. Zane rolled over and hugged the ground.

Something flipped over and over in the dirt until it stopped by Capt. Rendon.

Rendon looked up. He saw the object and picked it up. It was Pancho's pistol. Rendon did not understand what was going on.

Zane sat up and looked at his jacket. He landed in a fresh 'prairie muffin.'

The De Havilland was back up in the air and leveling off. Barney turned to look at Pancho.

Pancho was looking a little green and hanging over one side of his cockpit.

Barney smiled at this. Then he happened to look down and see the column of troops. He got an idea. He looked at Pancho and then at the troops. He would deliver the bandit leader to the Army -- that would make him a hero. Barney swung the plane around and did a steep banking turn.

This was making Pancho sicker and sicker.

With the turn completed, Barney looked for a suitable landing spot near the troops. He thought he saw one. He took the plane down.

As the De Havilland dropped toward the troops again, Capt. Rendon handed Zane the pistol. Zane looked up from the new decoration on his jacket's arm to see the plane coming back. Zane looked at the pistol and then at Sgt. Nester.

Sgt. Nester was being helped by a couple of soldiers and he was beginning to come around.

Col. Zane turned as the plane approached.

Barney was leaning out of the cockpit waving at the soldiers.

Col. Zane drew his .45.

"That's an act of war!! Shoot that bastard down!!!"

Zane fired several shots.

Other soldiers quickly pulled their rifles and fired on the plane.

"Sir, that is our own plane!" Rendon shouted.

Col. Zane was still shooting.

"We won't know that til we shoot it down!!"

The Colonel fired again.

The plane swung around to come back toward the troops.

Barney looked at the troops and then looked again.

The troops were firing their weapons at the plane.

Bullets whizzed past him. Barney ducked his head and maneuvered the plane away.

"Hey!!" Barney shouted, "What are you doing??!!"

The bullets kept coming and Barney put the plane into

another climb. Bullets pierced the wings and parts of the plane's body.

Pancho passed out in the cockpit and sank down in his seat.

The troops continued to fire at the plane.

Barney shook his head.

"I can't win!" he said.

He sighed a sigh of resignation and headed toward Mexico.

Zane fired his last shot.

"See! That plane is headed for the border."

Some of the soldiers were still firing as the plane flew off.

"Where else can he go — Sir?"

"Cease fire!" Zane ordered.

The firing slowly stopped.

The De Havilland flew away.

Zane put his .45 back in his holster.

"If that plane is sighted again, I want it shot down."

"But, Sir ...."

"That is a direct order, Captain."

"Yes, Sir."

"That may just have solved our little problem with civilian Linedecker."

Barney was shaking his head as he journeyed on. He looked to heaven for guidance. He felt like the Sweet Bird of Youth had just crapped on his birthday cake.

❧

THE BANDIT GANG WATCHED AS BARNEY SET THE DE Havilland down and taxied toward them. Pancho was still slumped back in his seat.

Barney swung the craft around and shut off the engine.

The bandits rushed the plane. Several pulled their guns and aimed them at Barney.

Emiliano was first among those who went to see about their leader. As Emiliano leaned over the cockpit to help Pancho, Emiliano was almost knocked backwards by the smell of Pancho's recycled breakfast.

Barney sat dejectedly alone. He heard the bandits help Pancho out of the cockpit and carry him away. Then after a couple of moments Barney heard several clicks very close to him. He sat up and looked around.

All Barney could see were pistols, rifles and shotguns aimed directly at him. He was surrounded by Emiliano and other bandits, all of whom had their weapons aimed at him. Barney's mouth dropped open, and he swallowed hard.

"Out, Gringo!" Emiliano ordered.

"What?" Barney asked dumbfounded.

"Out!!!"

"Barney climbed out, his hands high in the air. He stepped down to the ground.

"What did I do?"

Emiliano said, "You tried to kill Pancho!"

CHAPTER 20

"I tried to kill him? Are you crazy?!" Barney tried to explain himself to the enraged bandits who only knew that their general was returned to them disarmed and passed out. "He tried to kill both of us!! I brought him back — alive!!"

Second in command, Emiliano, didn't believe a single word of it.

"Move!!"

Barney walked off looking very miserable. He just couldn't seem to win.

FACING THE RIO GRANDE, OVERLOOKING IT FROM A HIGH bluff, sat DeDecker's General Merchandise Trading Post. It was a part adobe, part stacked stone structure which had been a part of the Texas Big Bend Country, almost it seemed, since before sand was discovered. The roof was rusted tin, the support posts were stacked red flagstones and both the open doors and windows were weather beaten wood and filthy glass. There were pack mules and one or two horses tied up to hitching rails at the hitching posts. In fact, a tired looking burro was tied up to a gasoline pump which appeared to have no other use.

An old Mexican Man slept in the shade under the porch while four children — Mexican, Indian, and Anglo — played together in the dirt.

Riding up from the river, still on the U.S./Texas side, was C Troop. Col. Zane and Capt. Rendon were in the led.

Zane pulled up in front of the Trading Post and dismounted. The stains on the Colonel's jacket were dry but very visible. Rendon dismounted. Zane turned to Sgt. Nester who was still on horseback.

"We'll stop here for a while."

"Yes, Sir." To the troops Nester said, "Dismount. Check your gear and fill your canteens."

As Zane and Rendon stepped into the shade, a tall, thin and ancient woman came out of the Trading Post. She had yellowed white hair and a soiled apron. This was Gertrude DeDecker, owner.

She looked over the scene and then spoke to Rendon.

"J. J., looks like you boys been chewed up an' crapped out by somethin'."

She got a whiff of Col. Zane. She leaned back.

"Smells like it, too."

"Gertrude DeDecker — this is my commanding officer, Lt. Col. Claude Zane."

"Mrs. DeDecker," Zane spoke in a very formal way.

Gertrude extended her hand to Zane.

"Th' name's Gertrude. I ain't now — ain't never been — ain't goin' t' be — nobody's Mrs."

Zane nodded his understanding and tried to smile. Why, he wondered to himself, were all the Texas people weird?

"There's a wash tub an' some soap out back. It'd be a good idea for you to go get acquainted."

"Thank you, — Gertrude."

Zane stepped out the front door and called, "Sgt. Nester?"

After he was gone, Gertrude turned back to Rendon.

"Whatcha want t' guzzle, J. J.?"

"Lemonade — sarsaparilla' — beer — anything cool?"

"Drop your carcass in a chair. I'll get ya' a beer."

"Deal."

Rendon sat as Gertrude stepped down into a cellar of the Trading Post. Rendon looked out the door at the troops.

The soldiers were dismounted and some were watering their horses while others were cooling themselves in the water trough.

Gertrude spoke from out of sight below the floor.

"'Spect t' see ol' Lurty come this a way anytime, now."

"Why's that?" Rendon called back.

"He come through here early this mornin' — headed up t' y'all's camp."

Gertrude returned with two beers from the cellar. She crossed to Rendon's table and put the two cooler mugs down.

"Here ya' go."

"Thanks."

Gertrude sat with Rendon while he downed half the beer in one swallow.

"That there's what'll make ya' fat."

"I think that track was laid a long time ago. A little late t' worry about that now. Now what's this about — Lurty?"

"You met him he told me. So you know how he can be."

"Oh, I know."

"He wants some Army help t' get his gal back."

"His wife?"

"Daughter."

"Th' one with the —." He didn't know how to describe large tits in a proper fashion to Gertrude.

"That's th' one. There's only one Addie. Lurty says she got herself kidnapped by Pancho Gancho."

"When was this?"

"Didn't say. Didn't stay around t' talk long. He must a missed ya'."

"We left on patrol at sun up."

"Well, he'll be along directly."

Zane stepped back inside the Trading Post. He was in his shirt and tie. He stood in the sunlight to dry his shirt sleeve.

"Come get ya' a cool beer, Col."

"Thank you very much," he said taking a chair at the table.

"Gertrude says Lurty is looking for us?"

"What is it this time," Zane said enjoying his first swallow of beer.

"That must be him comin' now," Rendon said standing and crossing to the door.

Zane looked down the road.

With a boiling cloud of dust behind him, Lurty rode toward the trading post.

"Looks like him," Gertrude said.

Rendon returned to the table.

"Sir, Gertrude says Lurty — Mr. Etheridge — is looking for us. His daughter has been kidnapped — by Mexican bandits.

Zane looked skyward. This was all he needed today.

CHAPTER 21

A few minutes later, Lurty was hot, dusty and angry as he stood talking to Col. Zane, Capt. Rendon, and Gertrude.

"If I knew where in the hell she was, d' ya' think I'd a' come t' you?!"

Gertrude got up and went to the Trading Post counter. Zane's shirt was now dry and he adjusted his tie.

Lurty went on, "I spent all night lookin' fer her by my ownself. She's been took, I tell ya'!"

"Mr. Etheridge, I am not authorized to go traipsing across a sovereign boundary into another country without proof."

"Damn!! If you had been at th' Alamo — Texas would still be Mes'can right now!!"

Zane stood to face Lurty.

"What you don't seem to appreciate is the fact that any intrusion into Mexico is a serious matter. It could cause an international incident."

"What d' ya' think gettin' my girl kidnapped is — tiddlywinks?"

"You also told us that one of our flyers had been kidnapped by Mexicans."

"Damn right. And ya' ain't done shit about that, neither!"

"Mr. Etheridge — "

"What's wrong with your hearing? I told you b'fore, it's Lurty."

"If you insist. Lurty — this morning we were attacked by one of our planes. Now the bandits don't know how to fly. The only way they could use one of those planes is if — if one of our own pilots — *defected -- deserted --* turned traitor and sided with the enemy."

Gertrude was shocked by this concept.

Zane glanced down at his second in command to make sure Rendon wasn't about to dispute what he was saying. Rendon looked at the table and took a swallow of beer. The Colonel looked back to Lurty.

"So, unless I have some tangible proof that your daughter is a captive — the United States Army cannot intervene."

"What kind of proof do ya' want?" Lurty demanded.

Suddenly a blouse last seen on Addie was tossed onto the table in front of Zane. On top of it was thrown Barney's leather flying cap and goggles.

Zane turned to see Emiliano standing beside the table with Beto behind him, smiling. It was Emiliano who had thrown the items on the table.

Rendon, as usual, didn't know what to make of this.

Lurty's eyes opened and he snatched up the blouse and examined it. He looked up from the blouse and pulled his pistol, aiming it at Emiliano.

"This b'longs t' my Addie. Where is she?"

Emiliano and Beto raised their hands casually as Lurty advanced on them.

Rendon stood holding the flight cap and goggles as Zane faced the two bandits.

"Sir," Rendon said, "this is Linedecker's flight cap. Here is his name."

Zane took the cap and looked inside where Rendon indicated.

"These are two of th' sons a bitches that tried t' stick me up th' other day. Where is she?!"

Zane put the cap down and stepped between Lurty and Emiliano.

"You have both Miss Etheridge and Lt. Linedecker?"

"Si," Emiliano said.

"Is my daughter all right?"

"Si."

"She'd better be!!!"

Zane pushed Lurty's pistol down and moved the rancher back a step.

"Let me handle this, please." the Colonel said to Lurty. Then to the bandits he said, "Are both of these people prisoners?"

Emiliano nodded.

"Who was flying the aeroplane this morning?"

"The gringo flyer."

"I thought so!"

"But Pancho had a gun on him all the time."

Zane's sense of triumph faded.

Rendon stepped forward holding Pancho's pistol he had picked up at the sight of the aerial attack.

"Is this your leader's pistol?"

"Si."

Emiliano reached for the pistol, but Rendon pulled it back. This was evidence, and he was not about to let it go.

Emiliano shrugged his shoulders. He didn't really care about the pistol.

Rendon asked, "What is Lt. Linedecker doing now?"

"The gringo is trying to take care of the senorita."

Zane disliked hearing this comment. But not as much as Lurty.

The Colonel said, "You're telling me — you have captured Lt. Linedecker, and Miss Etheridge — and Lt. Linedecker was flying against his will?"

Emiliano nodded.

"Pancho says —."

"Pancho? Pancho Villa?" Zane demanded.

Emiliano spat on the floor.

"General Pancho Renteria!" he said proudly.

"Pancho Gancho!" Gertrude corrected from behind the counter. "He's got a hook for one of his hands. One loco Mes'can if there ever was one."

"What do you — or your *general* -- want?"

"He ain't the brightest lantern in a deep dark mine, either," Gertrude added. "These two don't look too bright themselves."

"Pancho say, you can have the senorita, the gringo flyer — and his flyin' m'chine — for thirty thousand gringo gold dollars."

"What in hell does 'gringo' mean?" Zane asked.

"Us," Gertrude said. "Americans. Comes from the song cowboys sing to hush down their cattle — *Green grow the lilacs all sparkling with dew* — only they sing it 'green grow' or just 'gringo.'"

"Thirty thousand?" Zane asked.

"In yankee gold."

Lurty stepped around Zane with his pistol at his side.

"When and how does he want it?"

Zane turned on Lurty.

"The United States doesn't bargain with bandits!"

Lurty got his grit up and defied Zane.

"Nobody's askin' ya' to, starched britches. I wouldn't give thirty cents fer you. But Addie — my daughter —. Me — an' th' other ranchers 'round here — we'd pay. We'd even do it t' help them fly boys! They're th' onlyest ones that's done a damn thing t' help us!"

"You tell 'em, Lurty," Gertrude said.

"Thirty thousand yankee dollars?" Emiliano said.

"You bet your butt!! That's what you'll get."

Gertrude announced, "Count me in for a thousand!"

Zane was frustrated. "You can't do that!"

Lurty pushed Zane to one side.

"You jest stand over there an' watch!"

Lurty stepped up and confronted Emiliano and Beto with his pistol raised. "O.K., let's talk turkey!"

CHAPTER 22

E miliano explained the terms of the ransom demand to Lurty in the DeDecker Trading Post.

"You have three days to get the dinero."

"Three days?" Lurty couldn't believe what he was hearing.

"Three days. At midnight on the third day, Beto — him there — he will leave here with half the money. When he gets back to our camp — Pancho will release the senorita..When the senorita gets back here, I go with the other half of the money. By the next sunrise you will have the gringo flyer back."

Colonel Zane was more interested in government property. "What about the aeroplane?"

"He will know where it is and can take you to get it."

"What if somethin' goes wrong?" Lurty said narrowing his eyes.

"If something goes wrong on your part — we kill the senorita, the gringo and burn the m'chine."

"And if somethin' goes wrong on your part?"

"I am the last one to go." Emiliano said. "The senorita must be here before I go."

"You can bet your butt on that."

"She can tell you how the gringo flyer is and — anything else. If there is anything wrong — you can throw me in your stinking jail. Is it agreed?"

"Agreed."

⊗⅏⊗

THE FIGURE OF BETO RODE UP TO PANCHO'S CAMP AND dismounted in the dark. He was holding two sacks of money in his hands.

Pancho and the other bandits let out a cheer! Pancho took the money to count and a celebration began.

Later, satisfied with the count of the money, Pancho signaled one of his bandits who stepped outside and over to the adobe shack where another bandit stood guard. The first bandit opened the door.

Barney sat with his hands and feet tied.

Across from him sat Addie. Her feet were also tied as were her hands. However, Barney couldn't see them. She wore a poncho. It was a home spun Mexican blanket which had been folded in half with a hole slit for her head.

You, senorita, are free to go."

"Go?" Addie asked.

"The gringos have paid the money. You can go."

"Not until Barney is free," she said defiantly.

The bandit shrugged and closed the door.

When Pancho was informed of Addie's decision, he said, "We will carry her back in the morning."

Back in the adobe room, Barney said, "Addie, you should have gone."

"If I did, they might not pay to release you. They might just give you a bullet, instead."

Barney sighed and said, "I know — but that's what we're paid to do. To take a bullet."

"But if you do, then don't they stop your pay?"

Barney thought about that a second then said, "Yes. What a crappy deal."

They both sat back.

"How can you be an aeroplane driver and not like to fly?"

"It's called being a pilot. All it takes is the Army — and the help of a — *friend* — like Delbert Wascomb. If I ever get my hands on that —." Barney didn't finish. He was a gentlemen, act of Congress or not. Such words he didn't say in front of ladies.

"It's one of those dumb things you did?" Addie asked.

"Number three. I made friends with Delbert. He was the company clerk and I thought he might be able to get me off K.P. Boy, did he!"

"K.P.?"

"Kitchen Patrol – peeling spuds in the mess hall all day long."

After a moment he said, "Remember, the only reason I was even in the Army was my family."

"And their money?" Addie asked.

"Addie, I'd given up any idea of ever getting any of that money."

It's the first time Barney had called her by name. She was pleased. She was making progress.

"I wanted to get out of the Army," Barney said continuing his story. "Well, one night Delbert and I got drunk. He was telling me how the company commander would sign anything Delbert put in front of him. So I asked Del to write me up as an officer. I thought being a second looie – lieutenant would be better than a private. I told him to give me a bunch of medals, too. When I sobered up, I forgot all about it.

"Then two months later, when we were supposed to get our separation orders —"

"What's that?" she asked.

"Orders to get out of the Army. To be 'separated' from the service."

"Oh."

"Delbert got his orders, free and clear. He went home. But the Captain stepped up to me and pinned a set of gold bars on my collar. I was now a lieutenant. A 2nd Lt. The lowest form of life in the Army. I also got orders to report to Camp Kelly in San Antonio — for flight training."

The expression on Barney's face as he remembered those days was sad and depressing.

"Instead of getting out I had been extended three years. Three long years! And I was given a set of medals — none of which I ever earned."

"Two sergeants had to carry me to the plane the first time at flight training school. The instructor pilot was already in the rear cockpit.

"So, there I was, the most decorated 2nd Lt. in the U.S. Army. They couldn't afford to flunk me out. I tried to explain to them that it was all a joke — but nobody had any sense of humor. Nobody wanted to check the records."

"I still don't understand. If you didn't want t' fly, how could they make you?"

"Once they strap you in the cockpit — they can do just about anything they want to with you.

"I starting getting sick as the plane taxied and took off. My only solace was that I thought I had the perfect out. Whenever I get more than four feet off solid ground — I throw up.

"You get sick — floating in the air?"

"Violently. Then I made my last mistake — I threw up — and it all hit the instructor pilot – in the face."

CHAPTER 23

Although both were still tied up, Addie wanted to completely understand Barney's story.

"If you got sick so much — "

"Every time."

"— how did you become a -- pilot?"

"A mere technicality. On what was supposed to be my last instructed flight — I did what I always did. But this time the instructor got sick, too.

"Then he passed out — cold. Two thousand feet in the air and the only one who knows how to fly is passed out."

Barney looked at Addie to make sure she grasped the situation.

"I looked back at the other cockpit — and there was nothing there. I thought the instructor jumped out. But, since we didn't have any parachutes — he couldn't have.

"Now as much as I hate flying -- I hate crashing even more. So, to keep myself alive, I had to land the damn plane."

"Good."

"No, not really. By unanimous consent of the flight faculty, counting my last flight, they decided since the instructor was out cold, they ruled it a solo flight. They qualified me — gave me my wings — and they made me a pilot."

Addie burst into gales of laughter.

"Thank you very much for your understanding."

Diego, Pancho's third in command, pushed open the door. He crossed and cut the ropes on Barney's feet and hands. Next the bandit motioned for Barney to come with him.

Barney looked down at Addie.

Addie looked up worriedly.

"Don't worry," he said.

Barney tried to look brave and self-assured. He went with Diego.

Addie didn't know what to think. First she was worried, more so than before. Next she was also scared. She bit her lower lip to keep from crying as the door closed and Diego and Barney left.

Barney and Diego crossed the street of the abandoned town. They stepped into another building. The main room was lit by lantern. Barney was pushed across to Pancho.

Pancho gestured to the money on the table.

"They have paid for you, Gringo. I am sorry to have you go. There is a horse waiting for you."

"I thought Addie was to go first."

"Pancho changed his mind. I don't think your Army will pay to get you back." Pancho laughed. "I don't think they are too happy with you."

"Oh, I'll bet on that."

"So I send you first. The senorita will go when we get the rest of the money."

Barney tried to think of something — anything — but in the end he sighed his acceptance. He looked around again.

"Where is Doc? I wanted to tell him good-bye."

"He left this morning." Pancho stood. "You make Pancho laugh, Gringo. But now, time to go. I have money waiting."

Pancho stepped around the table. He put his arm around Barney's shoulder, walking him outside and over to where a horse stood saddled.

"I will tell you something about your flyin' m'chine."

"What's that?"

"I don't think they are very good. I don't think they will last very long. They are too dangerous."

"You should be in charge of our air corp."

Pancho laughed. "I don't think your Army would like that."

Barney stopped at the horse.

"It has been a real experience knowing you, Pancho."

Pancho laughed again. Diego helped or shoved Barney into the saddle.

"Follow the trail. The horse knows the way."

"You know, I don't like horses any better than I like aeroplanes."

Pancho laughed and swatted Barney's horse on the rear. The horse and Barney moved out of the camp.

It was a night of the full moon, but still the trail Barney rode was rugged and twisting. He looked to try to find the way. Finally he gave up.

"Horse, you do the drivin'."

He let the bridle go slack and the animal kept going.

Further up the trail, a dark figure was lying in wait. The trail took a turn around some boulders. Barney rode to the boulder where the trail was narrow and went along beside a steep drop-off. Barney pulled up on the reins and slowed the horse. But the animal was sure-footed and moved along with no difficulty.

Suddenly, from above him, Barney heard a voice speaking in a whisper.

"Barney."

The voice surprised Barney. He thought he was hearing a ghost. The voice spoke again. This time he realized it was the voice of Doc Starrett.

CHAPTER 24

From the dark Doc Starrett whispered Barney! Don't stop until you're around this bend. Keep riding!"

Barney did as he was told. When he did stop, he called out in a low voice. "Doc?"

Doc Starrett was crouched above and carefully climbed down to Barney.

"Don't act like you're talkin' t' anybody. Sit there like you're takin' a rest."

"O.K."

Barney sat steady, facing straight ahead.

"What are you doing?" Barney asked.

"I came t' tell ya' — unless you do somethin' — neither you nor Addie are gettin' out of this alive."

"What? They've already paid part of the ransom."

"Yeah. An' they were supposed t' let Addie go first. They ain't goin' t' let her go. Not till after they get through with her."

"That's not making any sense, Doc."

"Listen. Pancho never thought he'd get all he asked for. So he asked fer twice as much as he wanted. He's already got everything he really wanted."

Barney mulled this over.

"If he didn't expect to get the rest of it --."

"He even has a plan for — what's-his-name — Emiliano — the one who's waiting back at th' trading post."

Barney was having a little trouble keeping up with Doc.

But the doctor went on.

"Before your body is found — "

Barney didn't like the way that sounded.

" — Pancho thinks he'll get his army, cross th' river, shoot a few soldiers, and break Emiliano out."

"Then what are they goin' t' do?"

"I'm not sure. They were drawin' straws to see who gets t' kill you before you ever reach th' river. That was when I left. They like to make a game out of it."

"And how about Addie?"

The doctor stepped out of the shadows.

"Once they have word back that you're dead — they'll start sharing her around. Pancho'll be first. Then they'll all have their turn."

"I hate to ask this," Barney asked, "— but I guess you have a plan?"

Starrett stepped near Barney's horse.

"There's too many guns between here an' th' river. There's nobody that can ride out. Th' only way out —.

Barney got it.

"Is to fly out."

"That's right."

Barney sagged at the suggestion.

"I don't want to hear this. Whatever happened to your policy of minding your own business?"

Starrett frowned.

"I was the one who brought Addie into this world. If I'd been a real doctor — I might have saved her mother. I think I owe her."

Barney understood this.

"All right, if we are going to do something — it had better be quick — before I stop and think about it."

"Pull your horse over here in the shadows and leave her here. Come on with me and I'll show you how to get back to camp. I'll get Addie — you get the aeroplane ready."

Barney got down from his horse and dropped the reins on the ground. He put the leather reins under a heavy rock. The horse stayed.

Barney then eased himself up with Doc Starrett behind the boulder.

"Doc, we're all likely to end up dead in that thing. You realize that don't you?"

"Not if you're a good pilot."

"If I were a good pilot, I wouldn't be here."

"Well, you're the only one we've got."

"We'll have to wait until daylight t' take off. I need to see where we're going."

"Yeah, I figured that. They're still whoopin' it up back there. By sunrise they should be hung over — or knocked out. Anything else?"

Barney sighed.

"It's a little thing — but it could turn out to be important.

"What?"

"I don't know if we have enough fuel. We might be able to

take off — but —. It depends on how much fuel I used when Pancho went joy riding."

"Is there anything else we could use besides gasoline?"

"Kerosene."

"You can forget that. There ain't any."

"Then we might as well forget anything else. Whatever we fly with has to be pure — and highly refined.

"We can't do nothing. We have to try. Let's just hope we have enough."

"Yeah."

Starrett and Barney crept back towards Pancho's camp.

⚜

IN THE MOONLIGHT THE OPEN HOLE OF THE DE Havilland's fuel tank gleamed. A stream of liquid was being poured into the tank.

One of the bandits, his rifle slung over his shoulder, stood up on a rock beside the craft taking a piss. His aim was true and his target was the fuel tank.

Without moving his aim, he lifted a bottle of tequila to his mouth. There was only about one-fourth left in the bottle — he finished this off while he peed.

When he finished — both his intake and his output — the guard laughed and climbed down to the aeroplane where he put the fuel cap back on the fuel tank. Still laughing he reared back and threw the bottle. He heard it shatter somewhere off in the night. The guard then straightened up as much as he was able and continued to walk his post with as much dignity and sobriety as he could muster.

CHAPTER 25

That same night Emiliano sat at the table, picking his teeth with the blade of his knife at the trading post. Lurty paced the floor behind him. Rendon and Gertrude were also there waiting. Rendon pulled out his pocket watch and opened it.

The captain showed the time to Gertrude who nodded from behind the counter. Rendon started to put his watch away quietly when a word from Lurty stopped him.

"What's it say?"

"Twenty past four."

Rendon turned to Emiliano, who was getting nervous, but he didn't want to show it. However, it did show.

"She will come," he said assuring no one — not even himself.

Lurty crossed to Emiliano and leaned on the table.

"You hear me good, you goat-stealin' som-bitch! If anything happens t' my little gal — .

Emiliano lowered his knife and looked around the room

while he slipped his free hand under the table. In an instant he jerked out his pistol and leveled it at Lurty, fanning over towards Rendon and back.

"I don't like the way it looks myself. I think I will take the other half of the money and go."

"You ain't doin' shit till my Addie shows up here!"

"No, Señor, I have the gun. I think I will do what I want to."

Then from behind him Emiliano heard a metallic click. He froze in place as Lurty and Rendon looked toward Gertrude.

Gertrude stood behind the counter holding a sawed-off, double barrel shotgun. The twin barrels made for one of the meanest looking weapons ever seen.

"You s' much as blink wrong — an' you'll be on your way t' hell — in a bunch a' pieces!"

Lurty stepped over and removed the pistol from Emiliano's hand. Then Lurty took the knife.

"Capt'in, see if he's got anything else?" Gertrude said.

Rendon reached over and began searching Emiliano. The Army officer came up with a stiletto in one boot and another pistol from the back of the bandit's belt. Rendon pitched them on the counter. He returned and continued to search Emiliano.

A smaller pistol, two more knives, a garrote, a Derringer, a crude blackjack and a slingshot were all located.

Rendon stood up with his haul.

"This guy is a regular walking arsenal."

Gertrude held her anger and tried to stay calm.

"Lurty," she said, "it's your hand. You call it."

Lurty thought the situation over for a moment.

"This may be a trap here. But I got t' wait it out. Capt'in, best get on back t' camp. Tell th' Col. it's time t' go ass-kickin' 'cross th' river."

Rendon let go of his anger and took control of his better judgement.

"Good idea."

Rendon grabbed his hat. But before he exited, he turned back to Lurty.

"You sure you want t' stay here with him?"

Lurty nodded.

"I'll play it straight — jest on th' chance that ever'thin's still on th' level."

"You mean paying the money, too?"

"If Addie shows up all right."

Rendon shrugged and shook his head.

"If she ain't here by sunrise, I'll bring him up t' th' camp. But I aim t' see him hung."

The bandit tried to swallow and discovered he had a severe lack of moisture in his throat.

The captain understood.

"I'll swing by here b'fore we cross th' river."

Rendon left.

❀

Most of the bandits and camp followers were passed out, in one form or another. They were waiting on whoever was out there to bushwhack Barney to return with the word it had been done. Starrett crept through the camp.

He made his way to the shack where Addie was kept.

The guard on duty there was asleep, his rifle cradled in his arms.

Starrett moved quietly past the guard, pausing only when

the guard snored loudly. Then the doctor moved to unlatch the door as the guard drifted back off. Starrett eased the door open as quietly as he could. It turned out not to be all that quietly, but it was covered by the sounds of drinking, singing and snoring.

He stepped into the shack.

Starrett left the door open. He tiptoed over to Addie who sat in the same place — only now she was asleep.

Starrett cupped a hand over her mouth as he woke her.

Whispering in her ear he said, "Shhhhhhhh! It's me, Doc Starrett."

Addie recognized who it was and nodded. He removed his hand.

"I've come t' get you out of here."

Addie also whispered, "Why? What's wrong? Where's Barney?"

"Pancho ain't keepin' his end of the deal. Lean forward so I can cut you loose."

Addie did what the doctor requested. Starrett reached to cut the ropes loose off her hands — and a distinct — ripping of cloth was heard.

Addie's expression told Doc that the ripping was something of hers.

"I just split my pants, Doc."

Starrett just shook his head.

"I've been thinking you out grew those things a long time ago."

"I kind of like the way it feels," she grinned.

He cut her hands free with a pocket knife. Then he leaned down and cut the ropes on her ankles. He helped her stand up.

Addie was very wobbly on her feet.

"My legs are asleep," she whispered.

"Walk around a little t' get th' circulation goin' again."

As they walked, Addie straightened up and felt with her hand, under the blanket-poncho she wore. She indicated that the split was in the seat of her under pants. She covered her mouth to keep from laughing. Starrett shook his head again.

When he felt Addie could move well enough, he stopped her.

Into her ear he said, "Come on. Barney will meet us at his aeroplane."

"Ya' mean he's takin' us for a ride?"

"Let's hope it's not our last ride."

They crept out of the room and off into the dark.

CHAPTER 26

The bandit guard who earlier pissed in the fuel tank, was now hardly able to stand. He leaned on his rifle, dozed off to sleep only to wake with a jerk as his head dropped down.

As he jerked himself awake, he shook his head to clear it. Then the lights all went out in a snap when Barney crowned the guard in the head with a large rock. The guard crashed to the ground. Barney juggled the rock to one hand and with the other snatched the rifle up before it could clatter to the rocks. Barney looked around. All was quiet and clear.

Starrett and Addie made their way through the dilapidated town in the darkness. They almost tripped over the body of another passed out guard. They kept moving until they reached the De Havilland. They stopped at the body of the guard Barney had knocked out and both looked around. Barney was nowhere to be found.

After a moment, when they were beginning to think the

worst of things, Doc whispered into Addie's ear. "The next time you want to run away from home —."

Abbie whispers back, "Don't worry. I'll go north. Where is Barney?"

Barney stepped out and scared the hell out of Starrett. The doctor clutched his chest. Addie just grinned. When the doctor recovered, they eased over to the side of the plane.

The first shafts of sunlight radiated from behind the distant hills.

"Doc," Barney whispered, "you get in the back cockpit."

He turned to Addie.

"You'll have to ride in the front with me. I need the weight as much forward as possible."

"Are you saying I'm fat?" she glared at him.

"Doc?" Barney pleaded.

"You are a little — front heavy," Doc managed to whisper.

Of course, this pleased Addie who thrust out her chest under the pancho. She smiled

"Where do you want me?" she whispered.

"Put a foot here and here," he instructed her, "and climb in the front cockpit."

Starrett sat in the rear cockpit. "How are we for fuel?" he asked.

Barney picked up a tiny pebble, removed the fuel cap and dropped the pebble in. He heard it splash and was surprised.

"Sounds like we're half full. I don't understand it."

Barney turned to Addie as she getting in the front cockpit.

"Sit up here on the edge. When I hop in, then you'll have to sit on my lap."

Addie smiled at the thought, devilishly. "This gets better and better."

"Just do it."

Barney turned back to Doc Starrett.

"Doc, see the switch here?"

Starrett looked over the instruments until he saw the switch.

"I've got it."

"That has to be off — like it is now — while I spin the prop twice. Then switch it on — and pray this thing starts."

Barney adjusted the throttle to half way.

"If it doesn't?" Doc asked.

"Switch it off again. We have to go through the whole routine once more — until it does start."

Doc nodded.

Barney said, "We need to do this without talking. Remember, two spins -- off -- then on."

"Two off, then on."

Barney licked a finger to test the direction of the wind.

"Oh great," he said sarcastically.

"What?" Doc asked.

"We have to go all the way down there — turn around and take off this way. Otherwise we'll never get off the ground."

"Whatever, you say."

Barney leaned back over to Addie.

"We won't have a second to waste. When I get here and get in — ."

"Don't worry about me. I'll be right on top of you."

Barney didn't like the way she said that, but this was no time to quibble about decorum.

He walked around the wings to the prop and stood in front of the propeller. He looked over toward the hills. The sun was now rising and spreading its light across the flatland where the plane sat. Barney nodded his head.

Barney grabbed the propeller and spun it once. Then he repeated his action. He paused and looked around to Starrett.

Starrett flipped the switch. He nodded to Barney.

Barney spat on both hands, grabbed the prop and with all his strength spun it.

The motor coughed but did not start.

The sound of the De Havilland's motor stirred some of the bandits. Most awoke to discover their hangovers and fell back to the wherever they were.

Starrett flipped the switch and nodded to Barney.

Barney spun the dead prop once more. Then again.

He checked with Doc who flipped the switch on and nodded to Barney. The young flyer leaned into the prop and pulled for his full worth again. The motor caught and came to life. Barney stooped under the wings to the cockpit.

Pancho clutched his head with pain as he tried to sit up. He pulled himself up off a Mexican whore and listened. It was the airplane he was hearing. He forced himself to get up.

Barney climbed into the front cockpit just as the motor died.

CHAPTER 27

He stopped in mid sit. Addie bit her lip. Barney leapt out and ran back around to the front of the plane.

Starrett flipped the switch off and nodded to Barney.

Pancho came staggering out of one of the buildings. He was holding his head with one hand and his pants in his hook. He looked at his drunk camp. He heard the De Havilland motor being spun. Pancho grabbed a pistol from the belt of the nearest bandit still on the ground. He fired several shots into the air.

The bandits jerked up. Then they, too, heard the sound of the airplane.

Pancho rushed across the camp, firing his pistol and heading for the plane.

Barney had just spun the prop the second time with the switch off. He now shouted to Doc.

"Switch on."

Doc acknowledged, "Switch on."

Barney wasted no time in spinning the prop. Again it caught and the motor came to life. Barney raced for the cockpit.

Pancho ran up on the edge of a boulder looking down on the De Havilland. He fired his pistol at the plane.

Bullets kicked up dirt below the plane as Barney bounded into the cockpit and Addie slipped down into his lap. Barney strained to look around Addie as he throttled the engine and the craft began to move.

Other bandits joined Pancho at the edge of the rock and began shooting at the De Havilland. Then Pancho waved at his men to get to their horses.

The De Havilland gained a little speed as it taxied away from the camp. Addie was enjoying the ride. Barney was fighting the blanket/poncho she had on which kept flapping in his face. He looked around one side, then the other to see where they were going.

The bandits, led by Pancho, threw saddles on their horses. Pancho was the first one into the saddle, followed by Martin and Diego. Pancho yelled a curse at them and rode out with a few of his men with him.

Barney slowed the airplane down and turned it around. He did a double take at the approaching bandits.

Pancho and bandits thundered out from camp with their guns blasting away.

"Can we make it?" Doc shouted to Barney.

"If we can get enough power -- we can do it."

Saying that, Barney opened the throttle all the way and the De Havilland started to move.

The bandits raced toward the plane.

The tail was still dragging as the De Havilland gathered

speed -- then suddenly there was a burst of power and the plane lifted off with a jerk.

Starrett looked down happily.

Barney didn't know what to make of this. This plane had never had this kind of power before.

The bandits and Pancho were closing in but the bandits, some of them, broke off and moved out of the path of the plane.

Although it was in the air, the De Havilland was only a few feet off the ground. Barney, Addie and Starrett were dodging bullets as they went.

The distance between the bandits and the De Havilland narrowed and most of the bandits scattered. Pancho continued on.

The De Havilland pulled up into a steep climb.

All the bandits except Pancho pulled away out of the path of the craft.

Pancho ran out of bullets. He threw the pistol. The plane was over him and Pancho turned around and chased it.

He got right under the body of the craft and tried to stop the thing with his hands — his hand and hook. Unfortunately for him, his hook caught on the De Havilland's axil and Pancho was lifted out of his saddle.

The De Havilland continued on with Pancho dangling by his hook. Pancho looked down and was in shock.

His rider less horse and the other bandits were all dumbfounded as they receded below. The plane with Pancho attached kept rising.

Barney couldn't figure out what was happening. He looked over the side but saw mostly the lower wing.

Doc Starrett looked, then looked again, bursting into laughter.

Pancho now grabbed hold of the axil with his hand and was clinging on for dear life.

Barney didn't know what was so damn funny.

"What is it?"

Starrett pointed to Pancho.

"Pancho! He's caught on the axil!!"

Starrett laughed.

Addie looked around at Barney, then she leaned out to get a glimpse. As she did, Barney was caught up in the blanket-poncho which flapped in the wind. Addie couldn't see anything, but the wind caught the cloth and pulled it almost off of her in a single gust.

Clutching her hands over her breasts, in a futile attempt at modesty if ever there was one, Addie screamed and dropped into Barney's lap. Barney tried not to look — but this was an equally impossible feat. He couldn't help but pay attention to the soft, white, naked shoulders and a bust line — which would have been the envy of Mae West. Barney bit his lip and tried harder and harder not to notice. But everything seemed to get harder all at once.

Addie decided that she liked what was happening. Then — suddenly -- she felt something. Her smile changed to one of surprise. She looked back at Barney.

CHAPTER 28

Barney tried to look away, but his face was flushing beet red as he met Addie's eyes. Addie looked from Barney to down into the cockpit. She lifted with a slight flinch. A new smile began to cross her face. It got bigger and bigger. Then she closed her eyes, endured a moment of strain and pain — then the smile grew until it encompassed her entire being.

Barney was breathing harder and harder. His eyes rolled up into his head. Addie's breath also came in shorter and shorter gasps until she held her breath — then she wilted in a sigh of ecstasy.

Barney returned to normal and looked around as if to see if anyone noticed. No one did. He looked back at Doc Starrett.

Starrett was beaming as he watched Pancho.

"Barney!" he shouted above the wind as he patted the airplane.

"I didn't think she had it in 'er!!"

Barney turned away from Starrett and spoke to himself as he looked at Addie.

"She does now."

The De Havilland flew on. Pancho continued to hold onto the axil. Doc Starrett was enjoying the ride. Addie leaned over to the side of the cockpit to take a nap. Barney couldn't help but smile.

AT THE ARMY POST, CAPT. RENDON AND SGT. NESTER were mounted while Troop C stood ready to mount. The troop was in full battle gear. The door to the headquarters building was open and Col. Zane stepped out.

"Troop mount," ordered Captain Rendon.

"Mount," repeated Sgt. Nester.

The colonel stepped down to his horse. Before he could climb into the saddle, however, he stopped. He heard a sound. It was an airplane in the distance, approaching.

"Sgt. Nester!"

"Sir?"

"Are any of our turkey buzzards flying?"

"No, Sir. Your orders were that they all be grounded until further orders from you."

"Then what is that?"

Zane pointed in the direction of the sound.

Barney's De Havilland, with Addie, Starrett and the appendage of Pancho on the wheels, came into view over the mountains beyond the river.

"Is it a bird, Sir?"

"It's an aeroplane, you idiot," Captain Rendon said.

"It's — I don't know what it is, Sir."

The De Havilland continued to approach and it circled overhead.

Col. Zane, Capt. Rendon and the rest of the troop looked up flabbergasted.

One of the soldiers called out, "It's Number 13."

A cheer went up from the troops.

Zane was pissed.

Barney turned the De Havilland toward the river and began to descend.

The troop kept watch as the craft took a sudden dip.

"Sir, shall we go help him?"

Col. Zane isn't sure but finally said, "Yes."

Nester raised his arm to motion to the troops. As he stood up in his stirrups, he farted. Smiling the soldiers followed the sergeant, heading for the river while holding their noses.

The De Havilland kept descending lower and lower. Barney pulled back on the stick all the way. This woke Addie up as she felt his hands moving between her legs.

Barney shouted, "We've lost the air current. Hang on! We're going for a swim!"

Starrett braced himself.

Addie braced herself with her head on Barney's chest.

Pancho's feet began to trail in the river as the airplane headed for the American shore. Pancho climbed up on the wheels.

The De Havilland hit the water and flipped as the front end dug into the mud. Barney, Addie and Starrett went flying through the air – Barney had never remembered to instruct anyone about seatbelts. The three splashed into the river close to land.

Pancho came out sputtering and spitting river water as the

De Havilland came to a complete stop, nose down. It became evident that Pancho couldn't swim. But a rope was thrown out to him. He grabbed it and was pulled ashore.

Barney helped Addie up in the water. Starrett, too, surfaced. He peeled off his wet coat and slung it away.

He was laughing as he said, "What kind of landing do you call that?"

"If you can walk or swim away from it — it's a *good landing*."

"Agreed!" the doctor said.

The soldiers all rushed to help Addie out of the water, looking with ga-ga stares at the way the blanket pancho clung to her breasts. And she was aware of it as she brought her best assets to 100 % attention.

ॐ

LATER BARNEY, DRESSED IN A CLEAN UNIFORM, STOOD across the desk, from Col. Zane. The commanding officer slid a military form across to Barney. Zane offered Barney a pen. Capt. Rendon stood close by.

"Wait a minute, wait a minute! Right this instant — legally and officially I am out of the Army — a civilian?"

"Correct," Zane said without enthusiasm.

Barney looked over to Rendon.

"That's right," the Captain assured the young flyer.

Barney turned back to Zane.

"But I've still been awarded the Silver Star for bravery?"

"Yes, but those orders are still being cut."

"Then I've — distinguished myself in the military service of my country."

"I'd have to concur on that. Yes."

Barney looked askance at Zane.

"But — if I sign this — I'm back in the Army."

"You will be accepting a battlefield commission and be promoted immediately to the rank of Captain."

CHAPTER 29

"And you will be transferred effectively immediately," Zane added.

"That's part of the deal," Captain Rendon said.

"Far away?"

"As far away as possible."

"And how long would I be in for?"

"No longer than necessary." The Colonel asked Rendon, "What would you think, Capt.? A year? Two at most?"

"No, sir. More like — oh, six — eight months — maximum."

Barney still wasn't sure about all of this.

"Linedecker —," the Colonel said crossing from behind his desk to the closed door to the outer office. He put his hand on the door knob.

"It's either that — , he nodded toward the door, "— or *life*."

Barney made up his mind. He reached for the pen and signed.

"Now then, how do I leave — I mean get out of here?"

Zane returned to his desk, picked up the signed document and blew on the ink.

"You report to El Paso — A.S.A.P. There's a turkey buzzard fueled and waiting for you."

"Fly??!!"

"If you expect to leave — right now."

Barney nodded his understanding.

"Yes, Sir."

Barney saluted, Zane returned it, and Barney started for the door, stopping before he opened it.

Captain Rendon spoke. "Perhaps you might rather use the window."

Zane nodded. "Help yourself, Captain."

Barney stepped over and crawled out of the window.

Zane chuckled to himself as he put the signed paper in his desk. He then stepped to the window where he stood looking out. After a moment Rendon cleared his throat.

"What is it, Rendon?"

Rendon stood by the door ready to open it.

"Now, Sir?"

"Not yet."

Zane continued to look out the window. The sound of a De Havilland starting its engine was heard.

"Now." he said.

Rendon opened the door. Lurty and Addie entered. Lurty had on a suit coat and tie. Addie was in a white dress. Lurty carried a shotgun. They stepped over to Zane at his desk looking around.

"Mr. Ether -- Lurty. What may I do for you?"

"You know good'n well! I want that fly boy!"

"I beg your pardon?"

"Barney," Addie said.

"Lt. -- what's-his-name -- Linedecker," Lurty said.

"There's no one stationed here by that name."

The De Havilland was heard taxiing and beginning to take off.

"What?!"

"Captain Rendon?" Zane asked.

"That's right, Sir."

"Now, there was a Capt. Linedecker."

"Captain? Daddy, he's been promoted," Addie grinned.

"Unfortunately, Miss Etheridge, Capt. Linedecker has been transferred."

The De Havilland flew overhead taking off.

"Transferred? Where to?"

"He's been attached to a new group that is forming. It's all rather hush-hush, I'm afraid.

Lurty raised his shotgun at Zane.

"I said -- where?"

"Capt. Linedecker doesn't know it -- but his next duty assignment is with an outfit called -- The Lafayette Escadrille."

"Where in th' hell is that?"

"In France."

Lurty and Addie exchanged looks of dismay.

"France?" Lurty asked.

"France!" Zane assured them. "Yes. Capt. Linedecker has gone to fight the Kaiser."

Addie rushed to the window.

"When will he be back?"

"I'm not sure."

Barney was flying up in the clouds and he was as sick as

ever. But at least he could keep going. He tried to sing the first song that came to him as a way of helping himself.

"Over there. Over there.
Send the word to beware, over there.
For the Yanks are coming.
The Yanks are coming.
And we won't be home til it's over over there."

THE END

THANK YOU

Thank you for taking the time to read <u>Pancho's Pilot</u>. If you enjoyed it, please consider telling your friends and posting a short review. Word of mouth is an author's best friend and much appreciated. I love to write these stories but it's even better to sell some and know other people take some joy from them, too.

Thank you,
Jack R. Stanley

2 Free Ebooks

ChroniclesMURDER IN MULESHOE
There's a killer in town. Do we hunt the S.O.B. down or
throw him a parade?

GUNS ALONG THE RIO
Two fresh-off-the-ranch 17-year-olds join the Texas Rangers in
1858. What could possibly go wrong?

Two Free E-books@ http://eepurl.com/dKEi_Y

ABOUT THE AUTHOR

Jack R. Stanley is an award winning novelist, playwright, and screenwriter. As an officer and combat photographer in Vietnam he earned the Bronze Star. Yet he says, "When you're in a firefight and everybody else on both sides have guns while you have a camera --- you get to change your pants a lot."

After his military service he received both his M.A. and his Ph.D. at the University of Michigan in Ann Arbor in Radio-TV-Film. His doctoral dissertation was on the long running TV series GUNSMOKE. Stanley also received two of Michigan's most prestigious creative writing awards, The Hopwood Award, one for a one-act play and the second for a novel.

Still married to his gifted high school sweetheart, Stanley's first academic position was TV Area Head at The University of Texas at Austin's Department of Radio-TV-Film. He later moved to deep-south Texas and the Lower Rio Grande Valley for a challenging position with The University of Texas-Pan American. Here he taught Theatre-TV-Film for 30 years in the Department of Communication. He was Department Chair at then U.T.P.A. for 11 years. He did take one year out to work for The University of Alaska Anchorage as a visiting professor. Back in Texas, Stanley directed for stage at The University Theatre, produced and directed fifteen student-staffed, cast, and crewed feature films, writing most of the original screenplays.

He now lives in the Texas Panhandle. His webpage is http://www.jackrstanley.com. His rather long-neglected blog is *www.TheFictionWritersNotebook.com*

ALSO BY THE AUTHOR:

NOVELS

ALSO BY THE AUTHOR

Novels

[Westerns]

Guns Along The Rio

West Of The Frio

A Hard Line Between The Rios

The Mormon Marshal

Along The Outlaw Trail

The Gavel and the Gun

13 Steps To Hell

Massacre At Going Snake

Incident at Lajitas

Pancho's Pilot

Return to Redemption

Occurrence At Latigo

The Dove And The Hardcase

The Widow And The Hardcase

Some Men Need Killin'

Ode To An Outlaw

Hanging In Temptation

Bad News In Temptation

Gunfighters in Temptation

First Train To Temptation

[Political Fiction]

The Reluctant President

The Reluctant Incumbent

The Reluctant Candidate

The Elected President

The Impeached President

{Vietnam}

Through A Lens Darkly: Vietnam

{Mysteries}

Murder In Muleshoe

Corpse In Canyon

The Lovecraft Murders

Short Stories

TALES FROM THE ALASKAN GOLD RUSH

Klondike Justice

Dangerous Camp On The Kenai

The Winds of Skagway

Screenplays

6 and 10

The 7th Luger

Afternoon Delight

Angel's Revenge

Between Love And Murder

Blood Drive

Death Scene

The Defection of Grigori Dorsky

The Evil Eye

Fatty and Hearst

Gideon: The Horse That Saved Texas

Hell In Paradise

Hollowpoint

Holiday For An Assassin

Horse Thief Hollow

Incident A tLajitas

Love, Lust, & Life

Mom & Apple Pye

Pancho's Pilot

The Prometheus Peril

The Rape of Sarah Quinn

Reservations

River of Tears

Seven Reasons Why

The Thing About Love

The Texas Rattlesnake Murders

Too Good To Be True

The Vampire Rose

A Violent End

The Virgin Casanova

Plays

<u>Antigone In Texas</u>

<u>Cyrano</u>

<u>The Last Virgin From Las Vegas</u>

<u>The Seven Keys</u>

<u>The Unwed Widow</u>